Love Me Even When It Hurts 3

Jelissa

**Lock Down Publications and Ca$h
Presents**

Love Me Even When It Hurts 3

A Novel by *Jelissa*

Lock Down Publications
P.O. Box 870494
Mesquite, Tx 75187

Visit our website @
www.lockdownpublications.com

Lock Down Publications
Like our page on Facebook: Lock Down Publications
@
www.facebook.com/lockdownpublications.ldp
Cover design and layout by: **Dynasty Cover Me**
Book interior design by: **Shawn Walker**
Edited by: **Lauren Burton**

Stay Connected with Us!

Text **LOCKDOWN** to 22828 to stay up-to-date with new releases, sneak peaks, contests and more…
Or **CLICK HERE** to sign up.
Thank you.

Like our page on Facebook:

Lock Down Publications: Facebook

Join Lock Down Publications/The New Era Reading Group

Visit our website @ www.lockdownpublications.com

Follow us on Instagram:

Lock Down Publications: Instagram

Email Us: We want to hear from you!

Submission Guideline.

Submit the first three chapters of your completed manuscript to ldpsubmissions@gmail.com, subject line: Your book's title. The manuscript must be in a .doc file and sent as an attachment. Document should be in Times New Roman, double spaced and in size 12 font. Also, provide your synopsis and full contact information. If sending multiple submissions, they must each be in a separate email.

Have a story but no way to send it electronically? You can still submit to LDP/Ca$h Presents. Send in the first three chapters, written or typed, of your completed manuscript to:

LDP: Submissions Dept
Po Box 870494
Mesquite, Tx 75187

DO NOT send original manuscript. Must be a duplicate.

Provide your synopsis and a cover letter containing your full contact information.

Thanks for considering LDP and Ca$h Presents.

Dedication

To the greatest man I know, I love you with everything that I am. I thank God for you, for the wonderful man you are. Your encouragement and desire to see me push further in my writing career has been my driving force. Thank you for seeing in me what every other man has failed to see. You've loved me at my worst and loved me at my best. I'm forever yours.

To my baby boys RayJ & AJ, Mommy loves you. Everything I do is for you two. Thank you for being the greatest sons ever! Mommy loves you with all her heart.

Jelissa

Chapter 1

A'Leeseea "Leesee" Evans

I kicked my legs wildly as he tightened his grip around my neck, my vision already blurry, eyes wide with fear. I was seconds away from becoming completely hysterical. I tried to scream but was unable to produce any sound because of Savan's assault of me.

He leaned his face closer to mine and bit into his bottom lip. "I'll kill you before I allow you to leave me, Leesee. You know way too much. I can't let you ruin me. Never!" He applied more pressure to his stranglehold as his eyes lowered into slits and a bit of saliva dripped from the corner of his mouth down to his chin.

I humped my hips upward, trying without success, to buck him off of me. I didn't want to die this way. Not on the kitchen floor of the apartment my first and only love, Sharome, had gotten for us, hustlin' and making it happen in the cold-hearted streets of Harlem. Images of his handsome face continuously popped into my head as I lay there on the floor, completely helpless and at the mercy of the man I'd chosen to sleep around on Sharome with.

Man, karma really was a bitch.

I lowered my eyes as it became nearly impossible to breathe. My lungs felt as if they were filling up with ice-cold snow, my heart beat so hard in my chest I feared it would explode. I just wanted it all to be over. I didn't want to experience the pains from Savan and my poor decisions any longer, so I closed my eyes and prayed God would take me away quickly.

Smack!

I jerked my eyes open as Savan sat straight up and looked into my pleading eyes with anger written across his face. "Un-un, bitch, you ain't taking the easy way out. You gon' look me in the eyes as I kill yo' ass, because it didn't have to be this way, Leesee. We could've had it all. You and I could have been forever. But n'all, you wanna leave me. You want to ruin my life when you don't know what I've had to go through in order to accomplish everything I have. It's not fair, bitch! It's. Just. Not. Fair." He slapped me across the face repeatedly, then ripped by blouse completely off of me and threw it to the side of him. It landed next to the stove.

As soon as his hands left my throat, I took in a big gasp of air, struggling to inhale as much of it as possible before I was coughing as if I was smoking a blunt. "Please, Savan, I swear I won't tell nobody nothing. I'm sorry for making you feel like I would, but I won't. I have never been a snitch. Just let me go. You're killing me," I cried through a voice so raspy it hurt me to talk. I felt like the inside of my throat was bleeding side, though I didn't know if it was for sure.

Savan scrunched his face and continued to bite on his bottom lip. "We could've had it all, Leesee. I can't trust you, bitch, and you gon' die. But before you do, you gon' give me some more of this." He leaned all the way down and sucked on my neck, then bit into it so hard I could feel his teeth come together in my skin.

The pain was so bad I couldn't help screaming and flopping around on the floor. "Ah! Get off of me! Please!" I begged, feeling the blood slide out of the wound he'd just created.

He leaned all the way forward and licked it up as if he was a vampire of some sort, growling under his breath.

"Mm! Yeah, you so sweet." He licked at my wound again, then rubbed his cheek against mine in a loving fashion. "It's not supposed to be this way, Leesee. You're not supposed to make me obsessed with you, then run away from me. I'm supposed to own you for as long as you are alive. That was our agreement," he growled and sucked at my bloody wound.

His sucking only added to the pain. Not only was he hurting me, but I had absolutely no idea what he was talking about because he and I had never come to any form of an agreement like that. Savan was nothing more than a huge mistake, a fling I'd gotten too sexually addicted to. Nothing more than a regret I'd have for the rest of my life.

He licked up and down my neck while massaging my breasts, running his thumbs over my exposed nipples. "Tell me you love me, baby. Tell me you'll never leave me and I don't have to get rid of you like those other girls." He moaned, then sucked on the middle of my neck. His hand ran along my stomach and wound up in my panties, stroking my sex lips before I felt a finger penetrate me. "Open these legs and tell me what I need to hear. Now. Come on, baby. Please!" he growled with impatience.

I tried to shake my head, but was unable to because his face was there, sucking on my neck. "No, Savan. I don't love you. Now just let me go! I'm tired of this shit! Get off of me!" I screamed and brought my knee up with all of my might right into his nut sack.

"Argh!" he hollered before falling off of me and onto his side in obvious pain. "Fuck!" He closed his eyes and sucked on his bottom lip.

It felt like the apartment got ten times hotter. I felt the sweat sliding down my forehead as I made my way to my feet. Once there, I staggered a bit because my vision was kinda hazy and I felt light-headed. Savan reached out to grab my ankle. I jumped backward with my heart pounding. His other hand was still between his legs, his caramel face red. He looked like he was struggling to breathe, and though he was saying something, I couldn't make out his words because they sounded strained.

I bucked my eyes, looked around the kitchen, and ran full-speed to the knife holder and pulled out a butcher's knife. I was tired of being the victim, tired of this man taking advantage of me just because he could, tired of feeling powerless. So I stood there with the knife in my hand, struggling to breathe as the sun from outside shined bright into the apartment, illuminating me and making me feel as if I was being lit up by a spotlight.

Savan slowly made it to his feet with a scowl on his face. "Aw, bitch, you done fucked up now. Now I'm going to kill you, because I'm tired of playing with you!" He started to walk toward me with is fists balled. His eyes were wild and crazy. I didn't know what he had on his mind other than murder, and that terrified me. I didn't want to die. I missed Sharome so much.

I took a step backward with the knife in my hand as I felt the sweat slide down my back. I was shaking like crazy and wondered if I really had enough guts to defend myself against this man. "B-b-back up, Savan. Please. If you come near me, I'm going to stab you. I ain't playing, either. Now, just leave and we can forget this ever happened. I swear I won't say anything to anybody." Tears ran down my cheeks as I continued to shake harder and harder, as if I was freezing cold.

Savan stepped forward and pulled down the hanging rack of pots and pans that were in the middle of the kitchen for easy access. They clanged on the floor loudly. Then he pushed over the refrigerator like a maniac. "Ah! Bitch, stab me, then!" He shook his head from side-to-side, looked over to me with an evil smile on his face, then started to walk rapidly toward me.

I didn't want to think. I knew I had to move as fast as I could or this man was going to kill me so, as he approached, I didn't wait for him. In one motion I dashed forward and sliced the knife through the air just as he put up his forearm protectively. The knife cut into skin and left a big gash that immediately filled with blood. He yanked his arm away and hollered in pain. He held his forearm, looking down at it, then came at me once again with a sinister look written across his face.

Now I began to panic. I backed all the way against the pantry door, scared out of my mind. I didn't know what to do or what to think. I needed to protect me. I needed to get out of that house. "Please get away from me, Savan! Don't do this!" I begged once again, but my pleas fell on deaf ears.

His huge body blocked the rays of the sun that were shining through the window. Before I knew it he was standing in front of me. He grabbed my throat with one hand and raised the other, getting ready to attack me. "Die, bitch!"

That was all he could muster before I swung the knife upward and implanted it directly into his stomach with all of my might.

It felt like I was stabbing a big thick pillow. He released me, eyes big as saucers, and slowly looked down to where the knife was embedded deep within him. Blood oozed out of the wound, surrounding the blade. Savan looked at his injury, up to me, then back to the knife and fell backward, sitting on the refrigerator he'd knocked over. He pulled the knife out of his stomach and a rush of blood poured out of him, flooding his lap. He held the knife in his hand so tight his knuckles were white.

I placed my right hand over my mouth. "Holy shit. Savan, I didn't mean to. I'm sorry. I-I." I stuttered as my reality came crashing down on me. I didn't want to go to jail for the rest of my life. I didn't think I could make it in such a horrible place. The man I was led to believe was my father had recently been killed in prison. I knew if he was unable to survive in that type of atmosphere, then I wouldn't stand a chance. I had to call the police and get Savan to the hospital quickly.

Before I could gather myself enough to make that happen, he stood up and rushed at me while holding his stomach. I screamed, turned, and made my way out of the kitchen with him in hot pursuit.

"Come. Back. Here," he gasped.

I ran and tried to jump over the refrigerator in he middle of the floor, but my clumsiness caused me to trip over one of the open doors and fall flat on my face, hard. Seconds later I felt him pulling me by my hair, slinging me to the floor, and straddling me. My head was spinning. I felt blood leak into my eye, probably from where I'd hit my head. I looked up and into the face of Savan. He frowned, placed the knife to my throat, and began to slice me from one ear to the next, very slowly.

"Die, bitch! Die right the fuck now!"

I closed my eyes, and began to make my peace with this life. I felt the blade cutting through my skin, tearing it piece-by-piece, and then a loud, ominous bang.

"Nigga, what the fuck? Get up off of her!" came Sharome's voice before he kicked Savan off me with a boot to the jaw.

Savan flew to the side and dropped the knife on the floor. It slid into the hallway. Before Savan could understand what was happening, Sharome was all over him, landing punch after punch to his face. "You bitch-ass nigga! Who. The. Fuck. Do. You. Think. You. Are?" he hollered, beating him senseless.

Tia ran over to me and knelt down. "Oh my god, your throat is slit. He was trying to kill you. Sharome, he was trying to kill this girl!" she hollered, pressing her fingers into my bleeding neck.

Sharome had Savan on the ground, slamming his fist into the man's face over and over again. It was getting so bad that blood popped into the air with every hit. I wanted to tell him to stop, that he was killing him, but the vengeful side of me would not let that happen. Deep in my heart of hearts, I wanted him to kill Savan. I needed him to.

Sharome stood up and started to stomp Savan in the chest and face until he was no longer moving. Savan lay on his side in a bloody pulp, shaking as if he was having a seizure, and then he simply stopped.

Sharome ran over and knelt beside me with tears in his eyes. "Baby, are you okay? Please tell me you're okay. I need you so much."

The last thing I remember was trying to smile as I thought to myself that after all I'd taken this man through, he still loved me enough to save my life. Then I passed out from the blood loss.

Jelissa

Chapter 2

Idris "Shotgun" Wright

I scooted backward on my ass, reached into my ankle holster, and pulled out the snub-nosed .38 Special I kept there in case of an emergency. I cocked the hammer and raised it as the sun shone into my eyes, momentarily blinding me. Before I could see the multiple targets that were dead set on ending my life, I fired two rounds, *boom, boom*, just as the heavyset lady picked up her child and stepped into my line of fire. The first bullet caught her in the shoulder, and the second in the neck. She fell backward and dropped her child before lying on the sidewalk, lifeless. Her baby screaming at the top of its lungs.

I felt sick to my stomach. What the fuck had I done? I really didn't mean to. *How the fuck am I going to get out of this one?* I thought as the group of savages closed in on me with all forms of weapons in their hands. I shook my head. "Get back! Get back!" *Boom. Boom.*

Two warning shots let off in their direction. I was down to two shots, and there seemed to be at least twenty of them coming at me.

"Hey, he just kilt that girl with the baby. Somebody call Vino! Tell him this nigga just kilt his baby mama!" somebody hollered from one of the houses.

I couldn't tell where the voice came from. The next thing I knew, two black S.U.V.s rolled down the street and came to a halt right in the middle of it, then what looked like six men jumped out with guns in their hands and blue rags around their faces. The first thing I thought about was Kazi's murder. Kazi was a high-ranking Crip

I'd killed less than two weeks prior. I knew his crew would come back strong, but I wasn't expecting it to happen so fast.

The men jumped out of the trucks, aimed their weapons in my direction, and let their bullets fly rapidly again and again. There was no way for me to run. I was hobbled with nowhere for me to hide. I was caught slipping, and in the worst possible position. I aimed my gun at the only mark I knew for sure I could hit and let off the last two shots, catching him once in the chest before I felt all of the bullets attack my body at once. My last thoughts were of Leesee. I wished I could have seen her beautiful face one more time.

***

Two weeks later

Leesee

I adjusted myself uncomfortably in the hospital bed, hitting the switch on the remote that allowed the bed to rise up. I felt high as a kite and a bit woozy from the morphine they were pumping into my body. My throat was tight and felt like I'd swallowed a bunch of icicles.

Tia stepped forward and placed her open palm on my forehead, looking me over with obvious concern. "How do you feel, cuz?" she asked.

I looked up at the television that played over my bed. To my right side was the lunch tray I'd refused to eat. Four cups of Jell-O. I was over them. It had been the only food item they'd allowed me to swallow in two weeks, and I didn't know why because although Savan had sliced my throat, he'd not severed anything that would have caused me great harm. I felt like Sharome had gotten there just in time, or Savan would have. Thanks to my man, I was still alive, and I couldn't wait to get home to him. I owed him my entire life.

I winced in pain as I moved too fast and yanked the I.V. in the top of my right hand. It felt like my veins were being pulled. "I'm good, Tia. I'm just missing Sharome is all. I know I got a lot of explaining to do. I just hope he forgives me, and we can move forward from all of this. I need him."

Tia nodded her head in understanding and stroked my forehead. "You already know how he is. That boy loves the hell out of you. Y'all will be able to get over this. Trust me, I know this for a fact," she said, kissing me on the cheek.

There was a knock at the door, and then the nurse came through it, followed by two white women who were in plain clothes, though they had badges on each of their hips. "Um, excuse me, Leesee, but these detectives are here to speak with you again. I say again because this is their third attempt at trying. The previous two you were heavily sedated. I get the impression this interview is very important."

Tia frowned. "Do she need a lawyer present?"

The heavier detective stepped forward with her red hair pulled into a ponytail, smelling like she'd recently put out a cigarette. She shook her head. "No, she doesn't need one. We're simply here to find out about her attack. There has been a string of sexual assaults taking place in the Harlem area with this same signature, and we need to find out if this was another one of those. That's all."

Her partner stepped forward with a warm smile on her face. "Yes, you're not in any trouble here, Leesee. We're here to see if we can help you and help a few other victims in the process." She took a tuft of her black, curly hair and placed it behind her right ear before smiling again.

I sat all the way up and took a deep breath. "But I told y'all he never got a chance to rape me. He threw me to the ground and ripped off my top. I started to fight him, and that's when he produced a knife and placed it to my throat. When that didn't scare me enough, he began to cut." I swallowed and felt the pain of Savan's assault. I was trying like hell to remember everything Sharome told me to say. I didn't want to slip up and say the wrong thing. I knew that could get all of us in trouble, because I knew Savan was deceased and Sharome had gotten rid of his body along with Tia. I didn't know how or where, but I knew it was gone, and I wasn't supposed to give the detectives any information that would lead back to Savan or Sharome. I had to be smart and stick to the script.

The nurse put her hand in the air to stop us. "Let me get out of the room before you guys go any further, because I'm not supposed to hear any of this." She made her way out of the door with her wide booty switching from left to right. Her gray, curly wig bouncing with each step. She reminded me of my grandmother, and she had to be around the same age and complexion.

The heavier detective raised an eyebrow and looked Tia over closely. "Are you going to leave, too?"

Tia shook her head. "Hell n'all. My cousin been under heavy sedation. I'm gon' stay in this room and make sure her words aren't twisted in any negative way, and also that you guys are treating her fairly. I know how you coppers get down, and it ain't happening like that with her. She's a victim." She looked from one detective to the next and put her arm around my shoulders, holding me protectively.

I smiled and looked up at her. "Thank you, Tia. I don't want you to leave, either. I need your support. I want her here, so anything you guys have to say to me, you can say it in front of her. I have nothing to hide."

The heavy detective shook her head, reached into her shirt pocket, and grabbed a notepad. I could see her face turning red as if she was irritated. "I don't know why people always assume we're the monsters. We're here to make sure your attacker doesn't get away with this crime against you. But from the way you guys are carrying on, you'd think you were under the gun." She shook her head again, then exhaled loudly. "So, anyway, why don't you take us through the series of events," she said, stepping closer to the bed, ready to write in her notepad.

Her partner pulled out a small laptop, ready to type away. She also looked irritated, and it made me feel uncomfortable to tell them what happened to me, even though I knew I was supposed to give them Rome's version of the story.

They looked at each other, and then me.

I sat up further in the bed as Tia rubbed my shoulder. "Well, it's just like I've already reported, but I'll tell you again. I was coming from the lakefront on Thursday afternoon at around one. I pulled up in front of my apartment, got out of the car, and made it upstairs to my locked door. I put the key in the lock and was about halfway to turning it when I looked over my shoulder and saw a man running up the stairs. In a panic, I turned the key in the lock and pushed the door open in an attempt to get inside, but he was too fast. He caught me just as the door opened and pushed me inside of my apartment, tackled me to the floor, and pulled out a butcher's knife." I started to shake as I remembered how it felt to have Savan straddling me with murder on his mind. Then I remembered the feeling of the knife cutting into my throat and tears fell down my cheeks. Suddenly the room became too small, and I couldn't breathe. I needed some fresh air. I took a deep breath and struggled to get it inside of my lungs.

Tia's eyes opened wide. "Leesee, are you okay? What's the matter? What's going on with her?" she asked the detectives.

My chest heaved up and down, and I felt like I was having an asthma attack, though I didn't have asthma. "I. Need. You. To. Open. A window. I can't. Breathe," I said with my teeth cheesing together, sucking air through them.

Tia jumped out of the bed and ran across the room to the window, hoisting it upward. Then she ran back over to me with her chest rising and falling just as bad as mine. "That better?"

The skinnier detective grabbed my hand and held it. "She's okay, she's just having a panic attack. Some victims experience this when they have to tell their stories. She'll be okay. Just breathe, A'Leeseea, and take your time. Okay, sweetheart?"

I didn't like this lady using a term of endearment with me, but I nodded my head, nonetheless. "O-Okay." It took me about five minutes and a bunch of Tia rubbing my back before I was able to get ahold of myself. Once I felt I was ready to move forward, I told them so.

The heavier detective smiled weakly. "Okay. Now, after this person forced you inside of your home and threw you to the floor, did you scream or try to make any noise to alert the neighbors?" She scratched her arm, then flipped her hair over her shoulder while her partner waited for my answer with her fingers already in the typing position over the keyboard of her laptop.

I shrugged my shoulders. "I can't remember. I may have, but I do remember being so afraid that this man was going to slice my throat. So I think I went into survival mode and nutted up. But honestly, I just don't know. Why do you ask that?"

She scribbled in her pad and answered me without looking up from it. "Because if you screamed, then someone could've heard you and possibly saw your attacker once he left your apartment. So far we haven't gotten any leads to support a scream, so I just needed to know that." She exhaled and rolled her head around on her neck. "Can you tell us anything distinctive about him. His height, weight, color? Can you remember how his voice sounded? Anything?"

I tilted my head to the ceiling as if I was in deep though. "Well, he definitely had a Spanish accent. His words were of broken English. He called me *mami* more than once. He wore a half mask, so I was able to see his light brown complexion and curly hair. As far as height and weight, about a hundred and seventy pounds, five-feet-seven or shorter."

"Would you be opposed to coming down to the station and looking over some mug shots? When you're in a better physical position to do so, of course."

I nodded. "Sure, that shouldn't be a problem. I'm just hoping you find this bastard, because he knows where I live, and that's going to terrify me until you actually do find him," I lied and was beginning to sweat. I was hoping they were on their way out. I didn't want to answer any more questions.

But the heavyset detective had a lot more for me. "So, you say he never got the chance to penetrate you, but he ripped your blouse from your body, along with your bra and panties. What do you think made him stop?" she asked, looking over to her partner, and then me.

I felt like there was something weird in the air. I couldn't quite put my finger on it, but there was definitely something going on between the two of them, and I picked up on it. I was sure Tia did, too, because she lowered her eyes and slightly turned her head to the side, looking at the one with the laptop. "Look, he stopped because she fought his ass back just like she was supposed to. I don't know what y'all on, but I just saw the way you looked at your partner and gave her a look that said you two are up to something."

The heavyset one shook her head while the skinny one frowned.

I held my hand up. "Wait a minute, because I am not strong enough to go through all of this fucking arguing and bickering." I felt like I was getting a migraine. I fixed my pillow behind my back and sat up straight. "My cousin is right. I fought him with every once of strength I had, even after he put the knife to my throat and began to cut me. I believe since I wasn't a weakling he simply gave up and ran off to find an easier target. I can't tell you, because I passed out after he smacked me, jumped up, and ran out of the door. The next time I opened my eyes, I was in the ambulance, and my cousin was staring down into my face with tears in her eyes."

The detectives stayed there and questioned me for another thirty minutes before they left me with their cards and told me to get in contact with them if I had any new information. They told me to also get in contact with them when I felt I was strong enough to travel down to the station so I could look over some mug shots and photos of possible culprits.

In the end I had stuck to the script Sharome gave me as much as possible, and whenever it seemed as if they were about to trip me up, Tia stepped in and stood up for me. I was so thankful she was in the room. Had she not been, I don't know where things would have gone.

I stayed in the hospital for another week, and then they released me on a bright Thursday morning. I sat in the wheelchair as Tia rolled me down the hallway, talking a mile a minute. I was so happy to be leaving the building that I imagined it was what prisoners felt like when they were released from their institutions.

"Girl, all Sharome been talking about is you. He been driving me crazy. It's 'Leesee this' and 'Leesee that.' 'I'm finna spoil my baby when she get home. I'm finna give her the world because that's what she deserve.'" She sucked her teeth. "I'm so sick of hearing your name," she joked as she pushed me past an older lady who looked like she was having a hard time tugging her oxygen tank along. Every few steps she'd stop and take a deep breath. I felt sorry for her. I wondered if smoking was the cause.

When we wound up in the elevator, I looked up at Tia with a frown. "It sound like you got a li'l hatin' in your blood, cuz. Let me find out." I rolled my eyes and sat back in my seat.

By the time we made it to the front entrance, I was ready to jump out of that wheelchair and run out the door, especially when I saw Sharome standing outside holding a single red rose and a sign that read, "Baby's release day!!!" I had to laugh at that. As soon as we went through the double electric doors, I bounced out of my seat and ran into his big, muscular arms, feeling him wrap them around me. I don't know why, but tears started to run out of my eyes like a faucet.

"I missed you so much, ma. Word is bond, I been sick as hell without you. I thought they were never finna let you up out of there," he said, holding me tight. Then he lifted his head and kissed me right on my forehead. His thick lips felt soft on my skin, soft and a little moist.

"I missed you, too, baby, and I'm so glad to be back in your arms. I know we have a lot of talkin' to do, and I'm lookin' forward to it. But I do want to apologize to you ahead of time. All of this is my fault. I should've never betrayed you like I did. I deserve all that has happened to me." I lowered my head and felt like I was on the verge of breaking down. I felt sick to my stomach.

Sharome held me tighter and kissed my lips. "Baby, it's good. We gon' go over all that tonight, but in this moment I just wanna be happy you're alive and well. I would have went crazy if I didn't get there when I did. I don't know what I would do without you, Leesee, fo' real. It's been me and you ever since we decided to go that route." He put his arm around my shoulder and walked me further into the parking lot until we were standing in front of a 2019, black-on-black Range Rover. He chirped the alarm and then opened the passenger's door for me. As soon as it opened, I saw the inside was all red leather. It smelled like Somali Rose. I allowed him to help me inside before he closed the door and walked around to the other side.

Looking out of my window, I noted Tia was getting into the driver's seat of a pink-and-black Benz truck. The rims on her truck were also pink and black.

"Girl, I'll meet y'all at home. I gotta take care of some bitness, plus I know y'all need time to catch up. Expect me there at around one. A'ight?" she hollered before sitting down in the driver's seat. I liked that truck. I felt myself getting jealous and everything. Seriously, I wanted to know where she'd gotten it from.

I nodded my head. "That's cool. I'll see you then. But aye, before you pull off, who in the hell bought you that?" I hollered.

She laughed, slammed the door, and started to truck with a hum. Then she rolled the window down and stuck her head out of it. "Well, seeing that you was all in a compromising position during my birthday and what not, Sharome took it upon himself to buy me a gift that would be from the both of y'all. All I wanted was a Rav4, but he was like, 'N'all, you ridin' foreign.' So this is what I got for my twenty-second birthday. Later." She smiled and rolled up the mirror tints, making me jealous as hell.

Jelissa

Chapter 3

Sharome "Rome" Mills

Leesee sat on the bed, and I dropped down in front of her and took her small feet into my hands, leaned down, and kissed her toes one at a time. I loved this woman, and I appreciated her despite the infidelities on both sides. "I missed you so much, baby. I missed these perfect toes, and these small li'l feet. I feel like I gotta worship you for the next ten years or I'll never feel right," I said, kissing all over her li'l piggies.

She giggled, then pulled her foot away from me. "Baby, for real, I need for us to talk so we can get an understanding. It's been a lot of bullshit in the air, and we need to clear it. We can't sweep it under the rug with no understanding. It'll only make us weaker," she said, sitting back on the bed and crossing her thick thighs.

I stood up and took off my Polo shirt, tossing it on the bed before sitting down next to her in just my white beater. "A'ight, let's holler. But before we do, I want you to know you can tell me anything, and I ain't gon' trip. Ain't neither one of us completely innocent in all of this. I got some things I need to tell you, too. So, let's clear the air."

She swallowed and scooted out of the bed with her eyes wide open, pacing in front of me. "Damn, now you got me worried and curious at the same time. I damn near want you to go first 'cause I can't think straight wondering what you got to tell me. Is it something about another woman?" she asked with a look of distress on her face.

I shook my head and laughed. "N'all, we ain't finna do that. You gon' tell me whatever's on your heart, and then I'ma respond and let you know how I feel about it. After that, I'll take the stage and let you know what's good, but not beforehand. So, what happened with you and dude I buried?" I asked, really wanting to know what made her go that route with some old nigga. He had to be our parents' age.

She inhaled and exhaled loudly. "I fucked up, messing with him. I met him at NYU. He took a liking to me for whatever reason. We went out to lunch, and after lunch we were on our way to our cars when I was almost hit by a car, but he pulled me out of the street before anything like that could happen. And I think the way he snatched me up sparked something inside of me, because I have this need deep within my soul to be snatched up and dominated by a man, so when he did that it got me to wondering how he would do me in the bedroom." She said the last part so low I could barely hear her. "Long story short, we started to mess around, and all of the things Shotgun used to do to me, he did them, but it felt like when he did them, he did them out of love. I know that sounds crazy, but it's how I felt," she said, refusing to make eye contact with me. Instead she kept her eyes pinned on the carpet.

I felt irritated imagining another man snatching her up and getting her to the point it aroused her and made her want to sleep with him. I felt emasculated and lower than scum. "A'ight, but what would make you go out and mess with another nigga, anyway? Ain't I here trying to do everything I can to make you happy?" I asked, not under-standing and feeling weaker by the minute. I fidgeted around a lot on the bed, took my .45 out of the small of my back, and sat it on the dresser.

She nodded. "Yeah, baby. You are the best man I could ever ask for, and I love you with all of my heart. I guess I was just weak because the night prior to me meeting him, our sex sucked. Then, when I asked you to choke me a little, you made me feel so horrible. Like I was weird or something. I didn't like feeling that way. I can't help the way I am sexually. You have to blame that on Shotgun."

I ran both hands over my deep waves and exhaled. "Yo, I ain't tripping off what you need, ma. All you had to do was break that shit down to me. I'm willing to do anything to make you happy because you are my world. That man should have never been able to enter into the picture. You never gave me a chance."

She continued to stand with her head down, not saying a word. I felt my heart beating in my chest like I was starting to get heated. I kept seeing images of them together, rolling around in the bed with his hand around her neck, her moaning and screaming his name, begging for more. I felt like killing somethin'. I stood up with my nostrils flared. "Yo, so when you came home with all them passion marks all over ya neck and told me y'all ain't sleep together that night, y'all actually did, didn't you?" I looked her over from the corner of my eye.

She nodded her head slowly. "Yes, baby, and I'm so, so sorry. I didn't want to lie to you, but I didn't want you to leave me, either. I made a huge mistake messing with him. I should've never risked what we have. I just –"

I interrupted her. "And when you said you and him were through and you'd never sleep with him again, you wound up going back on that and fucking him anyway. Am I right?"

She exhaled and nodded. "It wasn't supposed to go like that. I went over there to end things with him, and when I got there he was all over me. And I tried to fight him off, but then one thing led to another and we were doing too much. I'm so sorry. I never meant to hurt you. I swear I will never do anything like that ever again. I hate myself for it."

I was pacing back and forth with my temper red hot. I kept seeing the image of me digging the grave for this nigga's body, right after me and Ramsey cut him up and burnt his body in a metal garbage can. I'd buried nothing but ashes, and in that moment if I could have dug them ashes up and kilt his ass all over again, I surely would have.

"Baby, can you say somethin' to me?" she whimpered.

I shook my head and continued to pace. "Yo, I don't know what to say. I mean, am I enough for you or not? What, you need multiple niggaz or somethin'?" I asked, confused as hell.

She shook her head. "No, it's not like that."

"Well, what is it, then? What made you mess with the dude's old ass?"

She exhaled and slumped her shoulders. "It's the dominating aspect, Sharome. I need that. Sexually, I mean. In the bedroom I need for you to dominate me and do me the way I need to be done. You're too nice. I need that animal in you, and I think I was afraid to ask you for it. And even if I had, I worried you would have been too afraid to give it to me. So I made a mistake with another man. Will we be able to move past this?" she asked, continuing to look at the ground.

I continued to pace in front of her. "All you had to do was teach me what was good, show me what you liked, and I would have broken my neck to please you. You know that. You're the first piece of kat I'd ever gotten, so I was just learning." I shook my head. "Yo, but I ain't even mad at you, ma. I just feel inadequate, that's all. I feel like I don't measure up, and it's messing with my pride a li'l bit. But it's good." I turned and walked up to her. "Yo, I forgive you. We can move past this. It's gon' take me a li'l minute to forget about it, but I will in time. Don't worry, a'ight?" I kissed her on the lips briefly, then turned my back on her and walked toward the bathroom. I needed to wash my face. I felt like I was on the verge of letting loose a few tears, and I ain't want her to see 'em.

She reached and grabbed my wrist. "Wait a minute, Sharome. You supposed to take the hot seat now. I need to know what you did to get even with me. I deserve to know. I told you everything," she said, pulling me back to her.

I faced her and looked into her eyes, feeling my own begin to water from all of the images going through my head of her and another man. I tilted my head backward and opened my eyes as wide as I could, hoping the air would dry them before any tears fell, and so far that was the case. I lowered my head and took a deep breath just as a tear managed to escape the corner of my left eye. I wiped it away and swallowed. "Look, Leesee, I slept with somebody else, too, but I don't want to go too far into it. I was wrong. I'm sorry, and I hope you can forgive me. That's it. That's all."

She looked at the floor for a long time and blinked tears, allowing them to fall off her chin. "Who was it, Rome?" Her voice was calm, yet assertive.

I shook my head. "Man, why do that even matter? It happened, and it's over. The bottom line is we both stepped outside of each other, and we gotta get past it. I'm willing to accept your apology as long as you're willing to accept mine."

She blew air through her nose and looked up at me. "How many times, and where was I?" She stepped into my face. "If you won't tell me who, at least tell me that," she demanded.

I ran my hand over my waves. "Like, two or three times, but it's over now. And I don't know where you were. I suppose with the dude or somethin'." I ain't mean to sound petty, but I didn't feel like dwelling on all of this shit. I didn't have it in me to tell her I'd slept around with Tia behind her back. I felt low even thinking about it. On top of that, I wasn't sure I hadn't developed some type of feelings for her. I mean they weren't strong, but I definitely cared about her a great deal.

Leesee smiled. "Yeah, okay, you right. Ain't no sense in me trying to dig around in your closet when I was doing my own thing as well. I say we move on, and we strive from here on out to have the strongest relationship and bond we possibly can. I love you, and I'm sorry for betraying you. Do you accept my apology whole-heartedly, as I do yours?" She looked into my eyes.

I looked down and nodded. "Yeah, I do. It don't mean it ain't gon' be on my mind for the next few days, but your slate is clean with me. I forgive you, and I want us to have a strong relationship from here on out."

Later that night, Ramsey scooped me up at about ten in his Raspberry Bentley truck. I hopped into the passenger's seat and he handed me a fat Dutch stuffed with orange and yellow Dro. He called it Starburst Loud. It was already lit, so as he pulled away from the curb I took a strong pull and inhaled deeply, feeling the smoke invade my chest, causing me to damn near cough up a lung. I let down the window so I could breathe and stuck my head out of it, trying to suck in the fresh air.

"Yo, the reason I'm scooping you right now is because we gotta holla at them Arian kids. I can't take what they did to you lying down, nah mean? So I had some of my hittas go and snatch 'em up, and we finna roll out there and take care of this bitness the Harlem way. You feel me?" he asked, taking the blunt as I handed it to him.

It had to be about seventy degrees outside with a nice breeze. I looked into my rearview mirror and saw the all-black van of security following close behind us. I knew every nigga inside of it was strapped with a full automatic. Ramsey didn't play games. He made sure his shooters came to overkill when it was time to get down. The best part about working for him was the security and respect our connection gave me throughout the slums of Harlem.

I swallowed my spit and could feel the stinging in my chest. I was high as a kite. My eyes were low, and the Jada Kiss coming out of the speakers was sounding like straight sauce. That fool Kiss always got me in the mood to be on some straight murder shit. "Boss, whatever you trying to do, I'm down wit' it. Them white boys tried to body me and Tia, so I gotta get at they ass. The fact you already snatched them up is music to my ears. Word is bond, if you wanna watch me body they ass to prove my loyalty, I'm game, big homie."

Ramsey smiled and nodded his head, looking at me from his driver's seat. "That's why I fuck wit' you, Sharome. You got heart, my nigga. And a nigga wit' heart supposed to be at my right hand at all times." He reached into his Tom Ford pocket and took out two pills, popping them into his mouth, grabbing his pink Sprite, and swallowing in large gulps. "You want a few Xans?" he asked, looking over at me as he turned the corner and the bright lights from 125th lit up his whip.

He was always trying to get me to fuck wit' them pills and that lean, but I wasn't interested in none of that. I was all about my paper, and I felt like that stuff just left me in a slumber. I wasn't trying to be asleep. I needed to be fully awake and on point at all times, so I shook my head. "I'm good, big bruh."

He laughed. "Mo' for me." He stepped on the gas and sped through a yellow light. I noted the van behind us did the same thing. "Yo, you heard about that nigga Shotgun getting lit up about three weeks back?" He laughed again and looked me over.

I shook my head. "Hell n'all. What happened? And who got 'im?" I asked with a smile on my face I couldn't conceal.

He turned onto the highway and leaned his seat back. "Them Crip niggaz got 'im. Say somebody put twenty gees on his head before they murked him. He bodied one of they homegirls. Almost hit her kid, too." He shook his head.

I felt like jumping up and clicking my heels together. In my opinion that was one less enemy I had to worry about. Now I had to find a way to get rid of Kazi, because he was just as deadly. "Yo, fuck that nigga, B. Word is bond, that stud was foul living. Karma was gon' catch up wit' 'im sooner or later. It always does," I said. "I wonder who put the bread up, though?"

Ramsey was quiet for a moment, and that threw me off a little bit. He looked at me twice but didn't say a word, so I knew somethin' had to be up. "Yo, what's good? You looking at me funny as hell." I scrunched my face and raised my right eyebrow.

He shook his head. "Yo, I guess you don't know, and I guess it's my place to tell you. But before I do, I just want you to know I love you, li'l homie, and I'm your family now. I'm about to put you on the map, like I been saying. You feel me?" he asked, looking to me and then back to the road.

I nodded my head, though I was starting to feel uneasy. "Yeah, I feel you. I love you, too, big homie, and I'm riding beside you until my last breath, kid. Now tell me what's good, bruh, damn."

He nodded. "A'ight, yo, them Jersey Crips put them chips on Shotgun head because he murdered your brother on some roof out there about a month ago. I guess that fool Kazi banged him on some fist-to-fist shit, and he couldn't take that ass-whoopin' lying down, so he blindsided him and popped him up. I'm sorry you ain't know, kid. I'm here for you, though."

I felt like a kid on Christmas morning, coming out of my bedroom to a tree full of presents. Not only was one of my enemies dead and gone, but all of them were. I felt like God was doing me favors I hadn't prayed for. I turned to Ramsey. "Look, I loved my brother, but it is what it is. According to him I was a dead man whenever he got his hands on me for choosing Harlem over his crew," I lied. "So it is what it is. What's good wit' these white boys? Why did they try to switch up the game all of the sudden?" I asked, imagining Kazi lying in a casket, blown away by Shotgun. I shook my head, then imagined

Shotgun in the same position. The only difference is his slugs would have come from members of my brother's deadly crew. After thinkin' about that, I wondered if Kazi had given the order for them to kill me on sight? I would have to ask Ramsey about what he'd heard. He always had his ear to the streets.

Ramsey took a long swallow from his pink Sprite – so long that when he finished the bottle was caved in on both sides. He smacked his lips and wiped his mouth with the back of his hand. "Them Asians out in the Bronx stepped on my toes with them. Offered to pay a little more, and you know how that goes in the game. Everybody always looking for the best quality of dope and the best deals. After hearing what the Asians were willing to pay them, they felt like I was getting over and demanded some of their money back, and you already know that ain't happening. Fuck I look like?" He curled his upper lip, reached, and turned up the Jada Kiss song that was playing on the radio.

I sat back in my seat and prepared myself for what I knew was about to take place with the racist Arian white boys. If I had to kill one of them, then I was cool with that. I didn't think I would feel any remorse simply because only a few weeks back they'd tried to kill me and Tia out on some farm where they cooked their meth. Had I not taken the leader, who went by the name of Randy, at gunpoint, I was pretty sure me and her would have been murdered by them.

Ramsey turned the system down and smiled at me. "I want you to fuck that big, white boy Randy over. Bash his shit. After all he put y'all through, that punk deserve everything he got coming, word is bond." He turned the music back up and nodded his head to the lyrics.

Chapter 4

Rome

Ramsey's crew closed in on me. I could smell the weed smoke and alcohol coming off of their breath and clothes. The heat felt like it was turned all the way up. There were rats scurrying all around the basement, so big they looked like raccoons. Sweat poured down my forehead, and my clothes were sticking to me. It felt like I had a million bugs crawling all over me. Randy struggled in his bonds with his hands tied behind his back and a big, silver piece of duct tape slapped around his mouth. Underneath I could hear him moaning and groaning, probably begging for mercy as blood dripped from his nose. To the left and the right of him, members of his crew were deceased, heads beaten in by one of Ramsey's goons. Every time I looked over his work, I felt sick to the stomach. The smell of their dead bodies was rank.

Ramsey stepped forward and put his arm around my neck. "G'on 'head, li'l bruh. Beat that cracker head in. He would've done the same thing to you had you not put that burner to his chin, kid. Make an example of this fuck-nigga, and let's g'on 'bout our bidness. You feel me?" he said before burping out loud and handing me the black Billy club.

I took it and swallowed my spit, looking down on the white dude. Suddenly I didn't feel like killing him. I don't know why, but a part of me felt sorry for him, especially after I saw the tears rolling down his cheeks. His face was a shade of pink. I reached and snatched the duct tape off of his mouth. I needed him to be disrespectful and say anything that would encourage me to do what I was being ordered to do. I didn't have that cold-blooded shit in me. I had a conscience and actually needed a motive to body a person. Back on the farm Randy made it seem like he was so damn tough and hated blacks. Real racist. I needed him to have that same energy right now so I could do my thing.

He looked up at me and took a deep breath. "What the fuck are you waiting on, you dirty nigger? If you think I'm going to beg you for my life, you're sadly mistaken. Fuck you, and fuck all the rest of these cotton-picking, no-good, son of a bit–"

Bam! Bam! Bam! Bam!

I felt myself being pulled backward as Ramsey went to town on the big, white man with another Billy club. I hadn't even gotten the chance to lay a hand on him. Two of his goons held me back. For what reason, I didn't know.

"This. How. You. Beat. The. Shit. Out. Of. One. Of. These. Punk. Ass. Crackers. Sharome!"

Bam! Bam! Bam!

Again, and again the Billy club smashed into Randy's head until blood was popping up in the air and all over the walls. Randy made these guttural sounds that were reminiscent of a pig being slaughtered, and yet Ramsey continued to beat him until his skull was caved in and blood poured out of the holes Ramsey had placed all over.

After he fell backward, Ramsey dropped the Billy club, and walked over to me. "That don't just go for them white boys, Sharome. Anybody cross you, that's gon' be they fate. Word is bond, you my li'l homie. Muthafucka cross you, they crossing this entire mob. Blood out, ma nigga. Y'all clean this shit up and get back to work," he hollered, picking up the bloody Billy club and wrapping his arm around my neck, leading me up the stairs and out of the apartment's back door.

When we got back in his truck, he grabbed a red rag and wiped his hands and face. His chest was heaving up and down, his breathing labored. I didn't know what to say. I kept on seeing the fate of those white boys in my mind's eye. I was hoping that since I didn't move on them right away, that he wasn't thinking I was soft or something, because that wasn't the case. I just needed to be amped up. Senseless killing wasn't my thing.

Ramsey sat the bloody rag in the cup holder in between us. "Yo, Sharome. I got this move I want you to handle for me out in D.C. I gotta ship a hunnit kilos of this meth up that way, and you the only man I trust for this job. You handle this, and I'll pay you a gee for each bird. That's a hunnit apiece. I'll give you fifty up front." He got out of his seat and grabbed a *Clifford the Big Red Dog* book bag off the backseat, sat back down, and opened it up, showing me the bundles of cash before handing it to me. "You game?"

I smiled and nodded. "Hell yeah. Just tell me the time and place, and I got you, big homie."

He nodded his head. "I got mad love for you, kid. Word is bond. Don't even sweat not having a blood brother no more, because you got a whole-ass blood family. Su-woo!" He hit his chest and growled.

After we got an understanding about the move out in D.C., Ramsey dropped me off in front of the crib after we hugged and shook up. I wasn't technically plugged in with his Bloods, but I had mad love for the homie and his crew of savages, and I would continue to show them my loyalty by honoring him. So I closed the passenger's door and made my way up the stairs just as Tia was pulling up to the crib banging Cardi B. Ramsey pulled off and hit his horn one time at her, and she returned his honk with one of her own.

I waited to put my key in the lock until she climbed the stairs and stepped into my open arms, where I hugged her like I hadn't seen her in a long time. She smelled like Fendi perfume. Her body felt soft and feminine, as always. I took a step back and kissed her on the cheek. "Where you been at?" I asked, putting the key in the lock and getting ready to turn it.

She grabbed me by the shoulder and pulled be back so I could face her. "Since when you start kissing me on the cheek and shit? I don't want that." She frowned with a disgusted look on her face. I could tell she was offended.

"Shh!" I put my finger to my lips. "It ain't like that. I can't be kissing all over you with my woman in the house, though. I thought me and you already had an understanding? You know I gotta start being one hunnit to her. You gotta respect that," I whispered loud enough for her to hear me.

She nodded her head. "Yeah, I guess." She exhaled loudly. "Well, from now on, if you gon' kiss me, you either kiss me on my lips or on my forehead. I ain't with that cheek shit. That for friends, and you already know how I feel about you. I love yo' ass to death."

She reached and ran her fingers over my lips, then sucked them. That completely blew my mind because I had never seen anybody do somethin' like that before.

"Open the door, damn. I gotta pee."

I was frozen for a few seconds, and then I simply shrugged off what had just taken place. I still had those murders on my mind so I was a bit shook over that. As soon as I opened the door, Tia shot into the house and left the door wide open for me to walk into, which I did, before closing and locking it. I kicked off my Jordans and made my way to me and Leesee's bedroom with the book bag on my right shoulder.

As soon as I got outside of our closed bedroom door, I could hear the smooth sounds of Jhene Aiko. I pushed the door inward. The further the door opened, the louder the music got until it was opened all the way and the scent of Jasmine whisked through the air and up my nose. I looked into the room, and standing right before me on the side of the bed was Leesee in a pink-and-black Victoria's Secret lace negligee. In her hands were two red pieces of silk. On her face was a look of determination. I dropped the book bag and stood there, looking her over from head to toe.

***

Leesee

I felt myself shaking all over. I was so nervous, and I wondered if Sharome would even want me after all I'd taken him through. I worried that since he knew another man had me, I would no longer look pure to him, that he would no longer desire me or look to me as his when I so desperately wanted him to own me in every single way.

I watched him drop the book bag and stare with his eyes wide open. I wondered if he was staring because he was shocked by how I greeted him or if he wasn't turned on by me. Man, my nerves were taking ahold of me for the worst.

On wobbly legs, I walked over to him and stood on my tippy-toes, kissing him on the soft lips. "I've missed you, baby, and this night I want you to own me. I want you to make me yours and do whatever comes to your mind, because I need you worse than ever before." I sucked on his lips and ran my hand under his Gucci button-up, looking to feel his stomach muscles, but all I felt was his bulletproof vest. It felt hard as a solid piece of steel.

He stepped forward and began to walk me backward into the bedroom, sucking on my lips loudly and gripping the cheeks of my booty. It felt so good to be manhandled by him that I felt myself leaking into my panties already.

"Mm, I missed you, too, baby. I need this body so bad," he groaned and ran his hand under my butt and into my hot crease, stroking my lips through my lace panties, applying just enough pressure to open my sex lips just a peak. I moaned and spread my legs as I continued to walk backward with him leading the way.

Just as he was about to kick the door shut behind him, Tia caught it and opened it with her eyes opened wide. "Damn, I guess I caught y'all at a bad time," she said, looking me in the eyes, then down at where Sharome's hands were cupping my backside. He continued to suck all over my lips.

"Uh! Yeah, girl, close my door. We'll be out there in a minute," I moaned as he tossed me on the bed and looked back at her.

"What's good, Tia? Is somethin' wrong?" he asked, unsnapping his bulletproof vest and letting it fall to the floor, revealing his ripped, muscular body inside of a black wife-beater.

She looked him over for a long time without saying a word. Then she shook her head, turned her back, and closed the door.

Sharome took his pistol and sat it on the dresser after taking the clip out. Then he grabbed a bottle of Purell, squirted it into his hands, and rubbing them together before coming over to me and kissing all over my lips as I lay back on the bed with my nipples aching.

"You musta got these li'l strips 'cause you need me to tie you up, huh?" he asked, kissing my chin and then the side of my neck that wasn't bandaged. Once there, he sucked the vein into his mouth and groaned loudly.

"Yes, baby. Will you, please? Can you please dominate me? I need you to, so bad," I moaned, squeezing my thighs together. I could feel my juices saturating my panties. I was so horny I felt like crying.

He picked up one of the silk strips of cloth from the bed and grabbed my left wrist, tying it to our headboard before grabbing the other one and doing the same thing. Once they were secure, he pulled at both wrists to make sure I couldn't get away, and I couldn't.

"Mm, baby, what you finna do to me?" I moaned and humped upward into the air. I wanted Sharome inside of my body so bad I was about to go out of my mind with lust.

He stripped off his pants, allowing them to drop to the floor, then pulled off his boxers, standing at the foot of the bed with his long dick hanging between his thighs. I watched it jump more than once before he grabbed it and started to stroke it up and down until it was standing all the way up like a brown cucumber. Only then did he crawl on the bed toward me and got between my legs, pulling my negligee upward and rubbing my kitty through the crotch of my panties.

"Uh, please! Don't play wit' me, Sharome. I'm begging you," I moaned.

He sucked on his bottom lip and smiled. "I miss this fat li'l thang right here, ma. I miss how hot it is on the other side. How I was always able to open that tight li'l pink hole up, stretching you to your limit." He laughed. "You asked me what I'm finna do? I'm finna punish this pussy until I bring tears to them eyes. That's what you need, right? You need that animal to come out of me?" He reached and yanked my panties down in one motion, then stood on his knees and stuffed them into my mouth before pushing my knees to my chest and slurping my sex lips into his mouth loudly.

"Uh! Uh! Uh!" was all I could muster.

He separated my lips and stuck his tongue as far into me as it could go, flicking it up and down before attacking my clitoris with his thick lips, sucking on her and causing me to scream at the top of my lungs because it was feeling so damn good. I couldn't control myself. More slurping and sucking. His tongue went in and out of me so fast and deep I felt like I was already being fucked my him. I spit the panties out of my mouth and screamed as my orgasm shot through me with full force. "Ah, shit!"

Sharome continued to suck and lick. He opened my pussy lips, slid three fingers into me, and started to work them in and out with all of his might. At the same time he slurped up my juices loudly. "Yeah, cum for me, Leesee. This my pussy, right here. Cum for yo' man. I love the taste of this shit!" he growled, fingering me like crazy while he sucked at my clitoris.

"Uh, uh, uh, I'm finna cum again, baby! Uh, I'm cumming again! Ooh, ah, shit!" I humped into his face as he ground it all into my middle with no inhibitions.

After I came the second time, he got on his knees and walked up the bed on them until his dick head was sitting on my lips. "Suck this dick, Leesee. Come on, ma. Make Daddy proud." He humped forward, causing my lips to separate.

I wanted to taste him so bad. The way he talked to me in a controlling manner drove me out of my mind. So I sucked him into my mouth and ran my tongue around his head. It tasted just a little salty. Precum decorated his head, and the feel of it on my tongue drove me nuts.

"Uh! Hell yeah, baby. Suck this dick. This yours, baby. I just gotta make you earn this pipe. Earn this dick, baby. I love my woman so much." He grabbed a handful of my hair and humped into my mouth while I tried my best to control my gag reflex. Sharome's dick was long and fat, full of veins. I was hoping he didn't get too excited and go too deep to the point where I'd start to choke, but I held my ground until he gripped my hair so hard it felt like he was pulling it out by the roots. The pain made me wetter. I needed him to do more and more of that, because the more pain he caused me, the more I needed him inside of my body. "Yes! Yes!" I moaned around his dick.

"Uh! Uh! I'm coming, li'l momma! I'm cumming! Ugh! Eat this, baby!" He humped his hips forward again and again.

Squirt after squirt of his juices splashed onto my tongue, further exciting me. I sucked and swallowed the thick globs until he released my head and backed away. He knelt with his head between my legs, biting all over my thighs before kneeling, taking his big dick, and slamming into my box like a savage.

"Uh!" I came at the feel of it.

Then his dick was plunging in and out of me like a battering ram, full speed, and diving deep into my center.

The headboard crashed into the wall back-to-back. It sounded like we were trying to hammer a nail into it. Our skins slapped into each others. His pipe opened me wider and wider. *Smack! Smack! Smack!* Sharome was digging me out and hitting my very bottom with no mercy.

"Wait, Sharome! Uh! Please! Wait, baby! Ooh! Fuck. Uh! I'm so, ooh! I'm so. Oh! Daddy. I'm so sorry! Uh! Uh! Help me! Shit! This. Dick. So good!" I screamed.

He pushed my knees further to my chest and started going to town like a maniac. With every plunge I could feel him go deeper and deeper into my womb, it seemed. His stomach muscles were popping, along with the veins in his neck. His gray eyes were lowered into slits. Sweat slid down the side of his handsome face as he murdered my poor little kitty.

Afterward he lay back on the bed while I sucked our juices off of his penis hungrily. He rubbed all over my naked booty cheeks. Every now and then he'd spank them and create a spark in me. It made me suck him harder and faster. I wanted this man so bad. I was happy he still desired me, that I was still his woman and we could get past the past.

Once we were completely finished, he held me in his arms while I rubbed his abs, taking pleasure in the ripples. "Baby, do you still love me like you did when we were back in Newark, or has your love changed for me a little bit? Be honest, and keep in mind I would understand if it had. I mean, considerin' all of the circumstances." Though those were the words that came out of my mouth, had he said he didn't love me as much as he did, then I would have been devastated to the point of serious depression. I loved this man, and I was so sorry I had betrayed him. I was willing to do everything I could to prove my unconditional love to him. I wanted our bond to grow stronger, and not weaken by any means.

He leaned over and kissed the side of my forehead. "You must not've believed me when I said I forgave you a hundred percent and I wanted to move on with our lives?" He kissed me again.

I sat there for a moment, hoping he would go on. When he didn't, I sat up and looked into his face. "Baby, that's not answering my question. You can't answer a question with a question. All that does in makes us go in circles. Now, be honest, do you love me any less than you did before?" I rose so I could look into his gray eyes.

He smiled, then shook his head. "N'all, I love you even more because we were able to get through our head bumps. I know this thing we have ain't going to be easy, but we have to do all we can to figure it out. We're only eighteen, ma. We got a lot of learning to do. Word is bond. Why, do you love me less than you did before, or somethin'?"

He peered into my eyes, and I swear it felt like my heart was pounding like bass drums. For some reason it felt like I was seeing him through new, more mature eyes. On top of that, I could not believe how fine Sharome actually was. He had me feeling some type of way all over again. I shook my head. "N'all, baby. I love you a million times more than I did before because you allowed for me to bump my head, and in the end you were still there to pick me up. I'm thankful for you, Sharome, and I swear I'm going to do all I can to never hurt you again. You hear me, baby?"

He smiled, then wrapped me back into his big arms. I snuggled up under him, and the next thing I knew I was out like a light, feeling like my relationship had been restored.

Chapter 5

Rome

I shielded my eyes from the sun as it shone bright in the sky, threatening to give me a serious migraine. It had been two full weeks since Ramsey had told me about the D.C. move with the hundred kilos of meth, and I was ready to get moving. He already gave me fifty thousand, so I was halfway there.

I stood in front of the Benz trunk as Ramsey loaded the final suitcase inside it and slammed it down hard. There was a light breeze flowing about that did little to rescue me from the humidity. The bulletproof vest across my chest had me itchin' like crazy, and I was trying my best to not think about it.

Ramsey walked up to me and gave me a half-hug. "Yo, son, be careful out there with them D.C. boys. This my second time fucking wit' kid an' 'em out there, and they've always been on the up-and-up, but them D.C. niggaz got a rep of being grimy as hell, so use your third eye and handle bidness accordingly. That's a lot of merch back there, so don't let shorty be driving all crazy and shit. I got seven hittas that's gon' follow close behind you, so if shit pop off, they got orders to protect you at all costs. My niggaz busting to murder. That goes for the police and all. Word is bond." He hugged me again and took a step back. "Remember, you gon' be meeting them at the old bus depot off Richards Ave. Old man Sunny waiting for you right now. Your contact gon' be a nigga named Vice Roy. Love, fool, and I'll see you in the morning." He patted me on the back and walked off with four of his security guards following behind him.

I wiped the sweat off my brow and fanned my face with my right hand before getting in the passenger's seat and closing the door. As soon as I was seated, Tia started the car and pulled out of the alley.

"You know how to get to D.C.?" I asked, putting my seatbelt around me. I wasn't trying to have the law pull us over for no reason at all. They was super petty out in New York, on that profiling shit.

Tia nodded her head. "Yeah, I used to drive out there every summer to visit my cousins. We good." She hit her blinker and made a left out of the alley onto a residential street.

To me it seemed like she had an attitude, and I needed to know why. We had a whole lot of dope in the trunk, and I needed to make sure me and her were on the same page. "Yo, what's good wit' you? Why I feel like you got a attitude or something?" I asked, turning the air conditioner up a little more. It was hot as hell. The vest made me feel like I had two sweaters on. I felt so uncomfortable.

She flared her nostrils and turned onto a busy street. "I want us to get some gyros before we hit the road. I got a craving," she said, obviously ignoring my question. I reached over and pinching her lightly on her inner thigh, right over her Prada jeans. "Ow! What the fuck is your problem, Sharome?" she screamed, smacking my hand away and rubbing the spot where I'd pinched. She swerved around a car, then made another right at the lights, taking time to look over at me with a frown on her face.

"Yo, I asked you a question, and you acting like you didn't even hear me." I looked her over closely and didn't care about how she was mugging me. "Now, what's yo' problem?"

She exhaled loudly. "You already know what my problem is, Sharome, and I don't understand why you're fronting like you don't." She rolled her eyes and pulled into the parking lot of Jahrome's East Coast Gyros, throwing the car in park. Beside her, Ramsey's truck full of goons pulled up.

I pulled out my phone and sent the head one in charge a quick text: *Getting somethin' for the road*. Then I replaced my phone.

I turned to Tia. "Yo, if I knew why you was acting how you're acting, I would have never wasted my breath asking you what was good. I'm too grown for this shit, and you is, too."

She curled her right cheek, exposing a hint of her teeth. "Ain't that a bitch? You really don't know, do you? Okay, well, let me just break everything down for you." She turned the car off and faced me. "I thought I was gon' be okay with just being the other chick, but I honestly can't be, and I know it ain't right. I wanna be your number one, and I want you to love me just as much as I love you. Every time I see you and my cousin together, it makes me sick on the stomach because I wish you were spending that time with me. That's the first thing. The second thing is you and I, Sharome, are having a baby. I could've beat around the bush and played games with you and not told you what was good, but there it is. I'm having your child, and I don't know what to do or what you're going to do, and I'm terrified." She lowered her head, then looked up at me with her eyes watery.

I didn't know I was holding my breath until I started to get lightheaded. Only then did I blow out a gasp of air.

"When did you find this out?" I asked, taking my seatbelt from around me and running my hands over my face. I started to imagine me telling Leesee this news, and I felt sick.

Tia looked out of her window. "Last Monday. I'm already seven weeks late, so I checked, and he confirmed it. I was gon' tell you, but I just didn't know how. Please don't be mad at me, because I can't take that right now. I'm already weak enough."

Before I could say something else, one of Ramsey's heavyset bodyguards came over and knocked on my window. I rolled it down with a mug on my face. "What's good, bruh?"

He wiped his mouth. "Look, I'ma go in here and get a bag of food and bring it to y'all. Do you want anything in particular?" he asked, looking from me to her.

She nodded. "Hell yeah. Tell them to put ketchup and mustard on mines, and two pickles. Grab two of them bad boys, and I'm good." She reached into her pocket and tried to hand him a $20 bill, but he pushed her hand away.

"Shorty, you good. I got this. What about you, kid?"

Even though I was blindsided by what she'd just told me, I was still hungry as hell. I needed to eat, and a gyro sounded awesome at that time. The scent coming from the restaurant had my stomach growling like crazy. "Bruh, just grab me one with extra meat and chili cheese fries. We both drinking apple juice, too, and good looking." I watched him walk off and turned back to Tia. "Look, I ain't mad at you. This just caught me off guard. You one hunnit percent sure it's my child, though?" I asked, just to make sure. I knew I'd kept a tight rein on her ever since we'd left Marcy Projects and she started to make the drug runs with me but a person never could be too sure.

She popped her neck forward, then turned to look at me with an expression on her face that said she was offended. She raised her right eyebrow and continued to look at me without saying a word, slowly shaking her head.

I frowned. "Shorty come on with all of these melodramatics. Just answer the question. Are you sure it's my child?"

She took a deep breath and continued to shake her head. "Sharome, ever since you came into the picture, all I've been about is you, even though I knew I wasn't supposed to be. But to answer your question, yes, it's your child, and no, I have not messed around with anybody else. I haven't been able to think about nobody but your ass. So I guess my question to you is, what are you going to do? Or what should we do, because I don't believe in no abortion, and I'm hoping you don't, either."

She reached over and tried to grab my hand, but I moved it away from her. I sat in my seat in silence. I didn't know how we were going to break all of this down for Leesee. I saw her going ballistic at even finding out Tia and I had been getting down behind her back. All of the sudden I felt lower than dirt.

Ramsey's goon came out of the restaurant carrying two big bags of food. The sunlight shone off his bald, sweaty head as he walked over to my passenger's side window. I lowered it and he handed me one of the bags with so much grease on the bottom of it that my stomach growled. Then he handed me the apple juices.

"Here you go, Blood. If y'all wanna chill for about ten minutes and eat before we get back on the road, let me know. That way we can eat, too."

I shook my head. "N'all, we good. We gon' eat this while we rolling. Time is money, kid, nah mean?"

He nodded, turned his back, and got back into their whip.

Tia started the ignition, backed the car out of the parking space, and made her way onto the highway. We didn't say a word to each other until we got past the first tollbooth. Then she reached over and stuck her hand in the bag, pulling out a handful of fries and stuffing them into her mouth. "Look, Sharome, silence ain't gon' get us nowhere. You gon' have to tell me somethin', because this is a real life issue. We're in a jam, and it has to be figured out. As a woman, I need to know what you're going to do so I can make the best choices for me and the baby. So, what's good?" She reached back into the bag to pull out more fries.

My head was spinning. It seemed like my reality came crashing down on me way too fast. I felt suffocated and a little dumb, because I couldn't think straight. On top of that, the sun was shining so hard through the windshield it was causing me to sweat even with the air conditioner blowing the way it was. But I knew I had to say something. I couldn't allow her to think I was going to treat her like a sucker or somethin'. I was more of a man than that.

"Tia, I got you. I ain't gon' make it seem like we didn't get down and do our thing. We never used protection, and I can remember coming in you every single time, so I gotta stand on this and be a man. I'm gon' have your back from here on out, but I just wanna let you know I ain't trying to lose my girl over this. I need to let her know what's good, but in my own time. I don't need you running ahead and telling her nothin'. You hear me?" I exhaled loudly.

She shrugged her shoulders and shook her head. "I ain't gon' tell her shit. That ain't my place." She switched lanes and lowered her sun visor. "I mean, I know she my cousin and all, but I feel like y'all have a stronger bond, so this news should come from you. Then, once she find out, I'll stand up to her and face the music. However, Sharome, I just want you to know that ultimately I want it to be us and our child in the end. I'm in love with you, and I know I'll be the best woman for you. You'll never have to worry about me cheating on you or doing none of the things she has. All I want to do is hold you down and be by your side whenever –"

"Yo!" I said, cutting her off.

She stopped mid-sentence and looked me over with her eyes wide. "What's the matter, baby? You scared the shit out of me."

I shook my head, looking at her with distaste written across my face. "Nah, we ain't finna do that. You told me what it is with our child on the way, and I got you. Trust and believe I'ma have your back every step of the way. You will never be in need of anything, and neither will our child. But as far as you trying to undercut her or say things that will pull me in your direction, that ain't gon' work 'cause I already feel like we betrayed her enough. To talk that shit behind her back in fakeness, and I ain't going for that. I love that girl, despite what me and you have done. So don't get it twisted. My loyalty is still to her first, and always will be."

Tia frowned. "Not when the baby come, though, right?"

I dug through the bag until I found my gyro, then I sat the bag on the backseat and placed napkins all in my lap in silence. I didn't know how to answer her question, and

I was trying to buy a little time so I could get my thoughts together.

"Well? You gon' answer me or what, because I need to know if you're going to always have our child on the back burner for Leesee? And if that is the case, then you need to start getting yourself together right now, because that's not how its supposed to go." She rolled her eyes and looked back out of the windshield, shakin' her head and mumbling something I couldn't understand under her breath.

I peeled the wrapper back, exposing about a quarter of my gyro, looked it over, and licked my lips. My stomach growled again, and I felt dizzy. "Look, Tia, I ain't got all of the answers. I don't know how I'm going to be when our child gets here. All I know is I love Leesee with my whole heart. We've been through a lot together, and I know this news is gon' kill her. You gotta let me process this, and then I'll be able to let you know what's good. I just wanna do the right thing. I wanna do right by her, and I wanna do right by you and our child. I'll figure it out. That's what a man does." I took a piece of meat from my gyro and placed it on her lips.

She smiled, turned her head slightly toward me, and opened her mouth, taking the meat and chewing it. "You gon' drive me nuts, Sharome. I swear you are."

A few hours later we pulled into the big parking lot on Richards Ave that used to be a Greyhound bus station depot. It had been shut down, and the company moved to another location. Old man Sunny was in the process of changing it into a Fat Burger, though he was only a few months in. As Tia parked the car, rain began to fall from the sky in a light drizzle. It also began to get a little darker.

I jumped out of the whip and jogged to the glass doors of the bus depot, knocking on them. No more than a minute later an old man with a long, black beard and a kufi on his head appeared with three gold chains around his neck. "What's good?" he hollered through the door on the other side.

Behind me, the rain was a loud pitter-patter on the concrete. "Yo, I'm here on Ramsey bitness. I got that work. I'm supposed to touch base with you, Sunny, and meet Vice Roy here in about a half an hour." I pulled up the collar of my jacket as the wind picked up, causing the rain to spray mist across my face.

Sunny sucked his teeth, then held up one finger. He pulled out his phone, talked into it, then held the camera out toward me before putting it back to his ear. I imagined he was simply showing them my picture to confirm who I was. I didn't know for sure, but it seemed like it made the most sense.

He started to nod his head real hard. Then he laughed and put his phone away before unlocking the door and letting me in. He embraced me with a hug.

As I gave a half hug back, I looked over his shoulder and saw two older men with graying beards, armed with revolvers in each of their hands and scowls on their faces. They looked me over like I was an enemy, and it made me feel uncomfortable. "Yo, what's good wit' dem over there, boss?" I asked Sunny.

Sunny broke our embrace and looked over his shoulder at his security men. He laughed. "Just my team on point. You know how it is, young buck." He looked me up and down. "So, you're Shotgun's son huh?" He looked over his shoulder at his crew. "You look just like that nigga, too."

I brushed the rain off of my forehead and wiped my hands on my pants. I didn't know what these old fools were up to, but I didn't like being linked in the same category with Shotgun. I knew my father had a whole lot of enemies. I shook my head. "I just found that out less than two months ago. My whole life I grew up thinking another man was my father, and I wish he had been. But that ain't the reason I'm here. Let's talk money. When will Vice Roy be arriving?"

As soon as I said that, I saw a pair of headlights illuminate the area we were standing in that had once been a Greyhound Bus Station lobby. There was still four counters were I guessed customer service had attended to the patrons who came in to buy tickets or whatever.

Sunny pointed. "That's him pulling up right there. Make sure you got all of your ducks in a row. You don't wanna fuck with Vice Roy. I'm sure Ramsey already told you that, though."

I watched as he walked to the door and opened it as two big, beefy, muscle-bound men stepped into the lobby, followed closely by a short, light-skinned man with long dreadlocks that fell past his waist. Sunny was about to close the door when two of Ramsey's men stepped up to the door and demanded to be let in. I waved them over. Each man carried two duffle bags apiece with the meth inside of it.

About ten minutes later I was setting a kilo of meth in front of Vice Roy. He cut it open on the side and took out a small quantity, playing around with the crystals before placing a portion on the counter, leaning his head down, and tooting up a thick line of it loudly. After he finished, he closed his eyes and pulled on his nose, smacking his lips together.

I continued to scan the room. It felt like there was no ventilation. I felt hot and irritated. "So, what's the diagnosis, Vice Roy?" I asked, wiping sweat from my brow.

He continued to pull on his nose, running his tongue across his teeth. "It's good. It's good, just like Ramsey said it would be. My only question is if he's still married to the whole thirteen apiece for each?" He sucked his teeth and stood up.

I nodded. "He told me y'all already had that worked out. You're supposed to snatch all two hunnit at thirteen apiece, so what's good?"

Vice Roy shook his head. "I got other investments that's pulling on my pocket strings. I can do twelve apiece. I brought $2,400,000 even. Tell Ramsey to take that, and I'll fuck wit' him in a few months. I'll double my order. He knows I'm good for it. Go ahead," he said, sucking his forefinger and picking up residue from the meth with it before sucking his finger again.

I picked up my phone and called Ramsey. He picked up on the second ring. "Boss, he screaming twelve instead of thirteen, saying he'll get twice as heavy next time. We good or not?" I asked, not trying to do too much on the phone.

"Fuck! I knew that bitch-ass nigga was gon' do that. Fuck!" he hollered so loud I was sure Vice Roy heard him. I looked over my shoulder at him, but he acted as if he hadn't heard, and I was thankful for that. I didn't want no problems wit' them D.C. niggaz. I just wanted to handle this bit of bidness and get out of there.

"Yo, tell kid to hit you wit' the loot, and y'all get up out of there. Twelve is good. Peace." He ended the call.

I nodded my head at Vice Roy. "It's good, homeboy. Let me see that paper." I said, walking over to him.

He smiled, picked up two briefcases, and slammed them on the counter, popping them open. Inside was nothing but stacks of hunnit-dollar bills.

I picked up a few of them and thumbed through them. After convincing myself it was all good, I closed the briefcases and we made our way out of there. I was thankful bogus shit didn't pop off. One thing for sure, I didn't wanna travel to D.C. no more. I just got a bad vibe from them niggaz.

Chapter 6

Leesee

It had been three months since me and Sharome had made up and forgiven each other for the things we had done. Things were finally starting to get on track, and I was feeling like my old self again, ready to enroll in the fall semester at New York Tech so I could pursue my child care license and get a degree in early childhood development. I'd always had a strong love for children ever since I could remember, though I didn't think I was ready for children of my own just yet. There was a part of me that just wanted to protect them and keep them from harm the way I wished someone would have done for me. I didn't know how far I wanted to go in the field, but at that time it was a serious interest of mine.

I woke up early one Saturday morning to a stabbing pain in my right side, around the area of my ovary. It hurt so bad I rolled out of the bed and fell to my knees in pain. "Uh! Shit! Who's here? I need help! Please!" I hollered and fell on my back before I fainted.

When I awoke, I was lying in a hospital bed with an I.V. in my arm and Tia, once again, stroking my forehead. I sat up and looked her over closely. "What happened to me? Why am I here?" I asked, and then I felt the stinging pain attack me again, causing me to lose my breath.

Tia jumped up and ran out of the room. "My cousin needs help. She just woke up in pain. I don't understand why y'all ain't got her on some type of morphine or somethin'," she hollered.

An east Indian nurse ran into the room and placed her hand on my forehead before checking my vitals on the monitor. "Are you okay? Tell me where it hurts." She said. looking me over.

I pointed to my right side. "Right here, and it's killing me. Y'all gotta give me somethin' for it. Please. It's taking my breath away," I said in between short gasps.

The nurse nodded. "Okay, we can do that, but unfortunately we have to be careful with what we give you because you are fifteen weeks pregnant."

"No, that can't be. I've been having my periods. That's impossible. And I surely can't be that far along and not have known."

She left out of the room and returned with a syringe, took the cord of my I.V., and injected the fluid into it. Almost immediately I felt more calm, and the pain subsided. I also closed my eyes, and the next thing I knew I had dozed off.

I remembered missing Sharome and praying he would make it back to town soon, because I needed him more than ever.

Two days later I sat on my bed crying tears of emotional pain while Tia wrapped her arm around my shoulder and kissed my cheek. "So, how do you know for sure it's Savan's baby and not Rome's? I mean, weren't you with him also around the same time?" she asked, making me feel sick to my stomach.

I shook my head. "Around that time me and Sharome were together, but he was on the road way too much. We were kind of stand-offish with each other, and on top of that we weren't screwing. The only person I was with was Savan. I keep records of everything, and I've already looked over my calendar for around that time. There was no sex between me and Sharome. So what should I do, cuz? I don't want to lose him over this. I thought all of it was behind me," I cried into her shoulder.

"Aw, baby, it's going to be okay. Don't worry, you're going to be okay. I think you should just tell Sharome the truth and allow him to make his own decisions. But if it's one thing I know for sure, it's that he really loves you with all of his heart, and not even something like this can break you two apart. Trust me on this." She kissed my cheek and placed her hand on my stomach, rubbing it in a circular motion.

I didn't know what to do. I was scared out of my mind. Then it seemed right on cue I heard Sharome's truck pull up in front of the house, blaring its loud music. The bass was so strong it made the house feel like is was in an earthquake, almost.

He turned it off, then I heard his footsteps ascending the stairs before our front door opened and slammed closed. "Baby! Baby, where you at?" he hollered, making his way down the hallway.

I wiped my cheeks and swallowed my spit as Tia sat back and looked me over, grabbed the wet Kleenexes off the bed, then stood up. She lowered her head as he came into the room, brushing past him without so much as a word.

He looked her over suspiciously, then shook his head. In his hands were four Saks Fifth Avenue bags. "Baby, I got you these cold-ass Eve St. Laurent fits that just dropped. I know that's yo' favorite designer. You gon' love these." He looked up and saw tears were streaming down my face, and he immediately dropped the bags and ran to the side of the bed. "Boo, what's the matter? Why are you crying?" he asked soothingly.

I swallowed. "Baby, I'm pregnant, and I don't know what to do. I'm scared you're going to leave me when I need you more than my next breath. I'm so sorry," I whimpered and broke into a fit of tears and coughs.

He frowned and knelt down in front of me, taking my hands. "Baby, what are you talking about? Why would I leave you? You're my everything. I need you just as bad. You're not making any sense."

I shook my head. "No, baby, you don't understand. I think you're going to leave me because of who the baby belongs to." I broke all the way down to my knees and felt like I was about to throw up. My chest heaved up and down, and I was so lightheaded it was causing the bile to rise from my stomach to my throat. I felt like I was on some type of carnival ride that kept spinnin' 'round and 'round.

***

Rome

I felt my heart skip a beat, then it felt like I was about to swallow my own tongue. I was praying she had not said what I thought she did. I stood up and took two steps backward, looking down on her. "What did you just say, Leesee?"

She buried her face into her hands and cried loudly, rocking back and forth. "I'm so sorry, Sharome. I swear I didn't know, baby. I swear I didn't know I was pregnant. I would have never allowed for this to happen," she sobbed.

I frowned. "What are you saying? Whose baby is it, then?" I hollered louder than I meant to. I was ready to snap the fuck out. I imagined her cheating on me again, and I knew I couldn't handle that. I didn't know what I had done wrong for her to still be sleeping with another man behind my back.

I started to feel insecure. Now that she was pregnant, I knew there would be no way we could stay together. I didn't think I could raise another man's baby. To look at her every single day and know she was nursing another man's baby in her womb would be too much for me.

She sat back on her haunches and wiped her tears away. "It can only be Savan's. He was the only man I was with while we've been together. I'm so sorry." She jumped up and started to walk toward me with tears streaming down her cheeks, both arms wrapped around her stomach.

I took two steps back, blinking as tears came from my eyes. I felt hurt. Assassinated. I felt like a knife had been stabbed into my heart and twisted again and again. After putting Savan in his grave, it turned out he was more alive than I'd thought. I lowered my head and allowed my emotions to get the better of me. Snot dripped out of my nose until I sniffed it back up, swallowing the mucous and shaking my head. "Leesee, dude been gone damn near three months. How is it you're telling me right now you're pregnant with his kid? How you know it ain't mine?" I asked, backing into the wall so hard my pistol fell off my waistline and into my pants. I was so distraught I didn't even attempt to retrieve it.

She took three steps forward, looking me in the eyes while huffing and puffing, her face so wet some of it dripped off her chin. She took a deep breath and blew it out, then tried her best to explain. "I-I-I went to the doctor because my side was hurting." She took a deep breath and blew it out. "They told me I was fifteen weeks pregnant. I hadn't missed my period, so I didn't know. They've just been irregular over the past few months. I swear, had I known, I would have gotten rid of it. I still will if you want me to, Sharome. I'll do whatever will make you happy," she sobbed, sounding as if she was on the verge of having an asthma attack.

I placed both hands over my face and hollered into them. "Damn, man!" I blew out a gust of air. I didn't know what to think or feel. I wanted to so badly tell her about Tia's baby, to confess and get it all over with, but I didn't feel like that time was the best time. I felt like I would have been doing it just to try to hurt her, which wasn't fair. The truth of the matter was I had made a mistake just as big as she had, but once again she was woman enough to tell me, and I had been too much of a coward to keep things one hunnit with her.

She walked up to me and grabbed my wrists, trying to pull them away from my face. At first I didn't let her. I had never allowed anybody to see me cry as hard as I was. I felt weak.

"Baby, look at me, please, because I'm freaking out. I need to know what to do. I'll do whatever you tell me to. Just tell me what you want. Please. I can't lose you. I need you so, so bad." She pulled on my wrists with all of her might, until my face was exposed.

I looked her in the eyes, then lowered my head. "Yo, it is what it is, Leesee. I'm still gon' ride for you until my last breath. I love you too much to leave you, and I'd never gee for you killing a kid. So it is what it is, I guess." I tried to walk past her, but she blocked my path.

"Look at me, Sharome. Look me in my fucking eyes and tell me you aren't going to leave me. Promise me this. Promise me you'll continue to go on loving me just as you always have."

Her eyes looked deep into mine. They were searching and going from side-to-side, seemingly to look deep into my soul. I tried to avoid them because I didn't know what to think or how to feel. I honestly felt sick to my stomach. I wanted to tell her about me and Tia so bad. "It's good, Leesee, damn."

She reached up and grabbed my chin, forcing me to look into her eyes. "Tell me the truth. What is it gon' be between us. Is it over or not? I'm not strong enough to endure any blindsides," she whimpered, and snot dripped out of her nose.

I pushed her hand away and took a step back, holding her by her shoulders at arm's length. "Like I said, I got you. This ain't gon' cause me to switch up on you. We can get through this. I'll support you in any way you need me to. You got my word on that." I pulled her close to me and wrapped her into my warm embrace, holding her while tears ran out of my eyes.

The harder I hugged her, the more I felt my emotions changing for the worst. She had been my everything, the first female I had ever loved with my entire soul, and in that moment just imagining her having another man's baby was the ultimate dagger to my heart.

After I broke our hug, I still could not look her in the eyes. I shook my leg and allowed my pistol to fall down and out to the floor. I picked it up and put it in the small of my back, wiping my nose with my hand before going into the bathroom and running cold water over my face.

Leesee followed me inside and rubbed my back while I was bent over the sink. "I meant what I said, Sharome. I'm willing to do anything that will make you happy. I'll go down there and terminate this pregnancy tomorrow if that's what you want me to do. You're my life. Nothing matters more than you do. Not even what's growing inside of me."

I know those words were supposed to make me feel better, but all they did was make me feel ten times worse. Every time she reminded me of what was growing inside of her, I wanted to kill somebody.

It didn't come as a shock to her when I grabbed my truck keys and told her I needed a little fresh air. She nodded her head in understanding. "Just make sure you come home tonight. That's all I ask," she said, following me to the door.

I threw my Jordans on, turned around, and hugged her just as Tia came down the stairs, putting on her light jacket. "Wait a minute, Sharome. Take me to the store since you're rolling out anyway. Or would that be a problem?" She looked from me to Leesee, then back to me.

I shrugged my shoulders. "It's cool wit' me. I was just finna roll around for a minute, anyway. Maybe I could use the company. I don't know, my head screwed up right now."

Leesee pushed Tia toward the door. "Yeah, girl, go wit' him to make sure he bring his butt home tonight. I don't want him out there doing nothing stupid."

Chapter 7

Rome

Tia dug her nails into my chest as I spread her legs, took my dick, and slid deep into her womb like a savage. I placed my right hand around her neck and squeezed gently, just enough to let her know I could cut off her air supply with practically no effort. Rolling my back, I stabbed into her pussy with reckless abandon. "Uh! Uh! Sharome, aw shit, baby! Fuck me. Fuck me as hard as you can," she screamed, opening her legs wider on the hotel bed.

I took her ankles and placed them on my shoulders, pounding into her with all of my might. Her sex lips wrapped around my pole, sucking it into her body with so much heat I had to close my eyes more than once and bit into my bottom lip to keep from coming. That pussy felt so good tonight for some reason. I felt like I needed it more than ever.

I released the pressure on her neck again so I could hear her moan some more and talk that shit that drove me crazy, speeding up the pace. "I'm finna. Fuck. This. Pussy. Until. It's. Raw. This my shit now!" I growled and slammed into her as hard as I could again and again. Every time I imagined Savan fucking Leesee, I took it out on her cousin. I made sure my dick was going deep into her belly. I even leaned forward on my left forearm so I could really dig into her. "Scream, bitch. Let me hear that shit!" I hollered. *Bam! Bam! Bam! Bam!*

"Uh! Uh! Uh! Uh! Aw, shit! Yes! Fuck me, Sharome! This. Yo. Pussy. Baby! Aw! I'm yo' baby mama now! Fuck me harder! Uh! Shit, I'm cumming, Daddy! I'm cumming. All. Over. This. Big. Ass. Dick!" She screamed and humped upward into me as she shook like crazy.

I forced both knees to her chest, killing that pussy with murder on my mind while the heat from her kitty scorched me and drove me crazy. I could not get the image of Leesee giving birth to another man's baby out of my mind. The more I thought about it, the harder I went on Tia. I grabbed her neck with both hands and squeezed. My eyes were still closed, imagining Leesee's face. My hips slamming forward with all of my might, digging deep into her womb.

She hit at my hands. "Ack! Ack! I can't. Ack! Breathe, Sharome!" she choked, scratching at my hands now.

I continued to pound into her with force, my eyes closed tightly, the pain in my heart almost too much to bear. I began to shake, and it wasn't because I was coming. I felt like I was about to mentally lose it. I pulled out of Tia, and flipped her on her stomach before I pulled her up by grabbing a fistful of her hair.

She let out a loud breath and arched her back. "Sharome, you trying to kill me. Slow down, baby. You fucking me too hard. You're going to hurt our baby. Ah!"

She yelped as I pushed her face into the bed, took my pipe, and slammed into her before I was fucking her with all of my might once again. Juices ran down her thighs, and along her inner knee. The slapping of our skins sounded like somebody was being slapped on the back over and over again. Her ass bounced into my lap, motivating me to go harder and faster.

"Uh! Uh! Uh! Sharome! Ooh! Daddy! You fucking me! You fucking me. So hard! I can't take this! I can't take this shit!" she screamed with her face in the sheet.

I grabbed another handful of her hair, pulling her head backward and lunging into that pussy, fucking it deep. Every time the soft cushions of her ass bounced into my lap, I felt like my dick got longer. I grabbed her aggressively and fucked her with anger until I collapsed, cumming deep into her hot womb, feeling her walls vibrate around my pole.

Afterward, I laid on my back while she took me into her mouth, sucking and growling around my penis head. "Mm, baby, I swear, don't nobody fuck me like you do. You do things to me that make me become more and more obsessed with yo' ass. I can't take it, Sharome. I swear. I'm losing my mind. I need you to love me a little more. Please," she begged, sucking me all the way down her throat, gagging, then trailing her tongue all the way up my pole, licking around the head. I'd cum twice down her throat and watched as she swallowed every drop of me. Though the head had me laced, I still could not get my situation with Leesee out of my mind.

Tia kissed her way up my body until she was straddling me, then she reached behind us and put my piece to her sex lips, squatting down, enveloping him. "Mm, baby. We ain't gotta do nothing else. I just wanted to feel you inside of me again. I love when you fill me up." She bit into her lower lip and lay her head on my chest while my dick throbbed deep within her channel.

I massaged her chocolate ass cheeks, squeezing them and pulling them apart so I could run my middle finger up and down her li'l hole. "Tia, I need to know you ridin' for me now, that you'll never make me feel what I'm feelin' because of this shit with my girl. Tell me you ridin' for me, and you gon' hold me down, ma. Word is bond, I need to hear that shit. Now!" I hollered gripping that big-ass booty.

She slammed backward into my lap, forcing my dick to go further up her pussy. It felt good, But I needed to hear those words from her because I was feeling so lost.

"Uh, baby, I'll never do you like she did. I love you way too fucking much. You're a good man." She licked the sweat from my neck and sucked on it, then bit me with her teeth. It made my dick harder.

"Uh! Tia! Yeah! Tell me you love me, ma. I'm hurtin' right now. Tell me you gon' love me through this shit! Please, baby!" I gasped, feeling my voice break up.

My tears had a mind of their own because as much as I tried to keep them within my face, I couldn't stop them from trailing down my cheeks. I loved Leesee so much, and I know I was wrong for screwing her cousin, but my brain was fucked up. How could the love of my life be having another man's baby? How could I be having a baby by her cousin and not her? Where had we gone wrong, and why wasn't there a way to go backward so we could really change the wrong paths we'd traveled?

Tia started to juice on my dick, bouncing up and down on it, squeezing it with her pussy muscles. Her fat ass cheeks were crashing into my thighs. I watched her perfect chocolate titties jiggle and shake on her chest, both nipples standing tall like baby pacifiers. "Uh! I love you, Sharome. I. Love. You. And. I. Always. Will. Uh! Shit!"

She slammed backward faster and faster, riding me like an animal. The bed shook like crazy. Her nails dug into my abs, then my chest, gripping me for leverage while she tilted her head backward, her face to the ceiling, riding me like a cowgirl on steroids.

I gripped her waist and made her fuck me harder. Every time she'd rise, I'd slam her down, making sure she took all of my pipe. "Uh! Uh! Uh! Uh! Ride this dick, baby! It's yours! Ride it. Ride me, li'l mama! Uh!" I grabbed a handful of her ass and started to cum in her in thick globs, splashing her womb again and again.

"Uh, shit!" she screamed, bouncing up and down like a kid on a pogo stick.

After we got out of the shower, I stood on the side of the bed, putting my clothes back on while she grabbed her phone off of the night stand and looked it over, shaking her head. "That girl been blowing me up. She wanna know where we are and why I ain't been answering my phone. She say she's worried. What should I text her back? Because she can see I read her messages now," she asked, standing up and wiggling into her Prada jeans.

Tia had one of them fat-ass project booties. Every time I looked at it, I couldn't help but get hard. Now I knew it was one of the reasons I'd gotten myself into trouble. That lust bug in me was strong for her. I didn't understand why, but it was too late to be trying to figure that out.

I shrugged my shoulders. "To be honest, I don't care what you tell her. We did what we did. I'm tryna see what's good from here on out. I ain't trying to think about her and I's situation. That shit fucking my mind up. I just need to chill," I said, throwing my beater over my head and pulling it down.

Tia texted something on her phone to Leesee, then bounced off the bed and walked around it until she was standing in my face. Once there, she wrapped her arms around the top of my neck, stood on her tippy-toes just like Leesee, and kissed me on the lips, sucking them into her mouth loudly, then licking all over them. "Mm. Baby, you don't have to worry about y'all situation no more. I got it from here. I'll do everything you need me to do. I'll submit like she never has, and you'll never have to worry about another man climbin' between my legs because I belong to you and only you. Isn't that what you want, baby? Huh? Isn't that what you wanted from her, but she couldn't give that to you?" She looked into my eyes.

I swallowed and felt sick to my stomach. I hated to be reminded of what Leesee could not do. Now I was supposed to just sit back and accept the fact she was having Savan's baby. I really didn't know if I had that in me.

I turned my back on Tia, walked to the night table, and put my pistol on my hip. "Yo, even though it's killing me, I still love her, and I gotta make sure she's okay at all times. You don't know what we've been through. I love that girl with all of my heart. It's just the fucking baby is so much. That means for the rest of my life I have to be reminded of when she cheated on me, when I wasn't good enough to satisfy her. That is killing me, Tia." I ran my hand over my face and shook my head.

Tia stepped in front of me and rested her hands on my shoulders. "But Sharome, we did the same thing. I mean, once she finds out this baby is yours, she's bound to feel the same way. Then what, huh? You'll both go on resenting each other. What type of relationship is that, huh?" she asked, looking up to me with those pretty brown eyes. "Just imagine it, Sharome. You know she gon' get her revenge again. She definitely finna be fucking another older nigga, because that's all she really likes. You'll be a fool to think otherwise."

I exhaled. "Yo, I ain't trying to think like that. I don't even know what I wanna do right now. My brain scrambled. All I know is I love her, Tia. Can't you give me some type of positive advice that'll help me and her relationship get stronger? I can't lose my baby. I don't wanna give up, but I feel like we've both sinned against each other one too many times. Damn!" I slammed my back against the wall and tilted my head backward, inhaling and exhaling loudly. Every time I saw Leesee's beautiful face, I felt weaker and weaker. I honestly didn't know what to do. My age of eighteen was kicking in full force, because I felt immature when it came to matters of the heart. I just wanted it to go back to the days before we left Jersey, when all we had to depend on was us.

Tia turned her back to me and balled her fists. She shook her head and exhaled loudly, took a couple of paces forward, holding her lower back with both hands before turning around to face me. "So, here I am telling you how much I care about you and how much I am willing to submit to you and only you, and that's your response? You shit on me like that when ever since the day I met you I've been nothing less than loyal to yo' ass, and my cousin been fucking off on you since the day she left her mother's house? She couldn't wait to break free, but you too stupid to see that. That girl don't give a fuck about you. All she cares about is the money you bring in. If not for that, she'da left you a long time ago for a more distinguished gentleman. Meanwhile, I fell for you so fast I was willing to go on the dangerous-ass road beside you just so I could be near you and make sure you're okay, or if you met that reaper, I'd be right beside you, because you are my life. For real, Sharome. I'll kill somebody over you. Why can't you just be with me and be happy? Or at the very least make me your number one and make her your side bitch? I've played that role long enough. Ain't it about time I get a raise in stature?" She flared her nose, then very slowly looked up at me with a look of extreme irritation.

I didn't even have the words to go back and forth with her. Like I said before, my mind was clouded by all of our current circumstances. I had never been more lost in my life.

I fitted my feet into my Jordans and tucked in the laces before standing back up and looking her over without saying a word. A part of me honored what she was saying, but another part of me couldn't really get down with the fact she was shitting on her blood cousin like she was. All for me. It made me question her loyalty, and I wondered how long it would take before she'd turn her back on me. I loved Leesee way too much to take a gamble on Tia, though at the same time I didn't know if I was strong enough to be able to endure losing both Tia's and Leesee's love. I had never had anyone love me my entire life prior to Leesee, and I didn't want to go back to that life. It sucked, and every day I woke up hoping to die before I closed my eyes.

"So, you ain't got shit to say right now? You just gon' look at me with a dumbass expression on your face, huh?" She sucked her teeth and waved me off. "Alright then. Whatever, Sharome. Just know I love you, and I will never stop. Whenever you're ready to settle down with a real woman, one that will never cheat on you, that will always put you first, then please let me know, baby. Because I'll be close by, waiting on my moment."

She walked over to me and wrapped her arms around my waist, lying her head on my chest.

Chapter 8

Tiana "Tia" Jones

I turned off the ignition, just as the lightning flashed through the sky. Seconds later there was a loud bang, and it seemed like the rain started to crash against my truck with full force. I grabbed the umbrella off my passenger's seat, cracked open my driver's door, then jumped out of the truck, running full speed across the street with the umbrella opened over my head. All around me was the constant sound of water hitting the ground. I ran until I was all the way inside of the big project building on 129th. Once in, I closed my umbrella and shook it out, walking to the stairwell where I took them two at a time.

It had been a full week since me and Sharome had our sex romp inside of the Hilton, and since then he'd finally exposed to Leesee the fact Shotgun and Kazi had been murdered three months prior. I didn't know what his logic was with waiting so long to tell her, but at receiving the news she fell to her knees and started to thank the Lord up above.

I continued to rush up the flight of stairs until I made it to the thirteenth floor. Once there, I stepped into the hallway and looked around. It smelled like strong coffee, piss, and feces. There were rats running up and down the hall while roaches crawled all over the walls that were painted with graffiti. I shook my head and stomped by foot at two big rats that looked like they were on their way in my direction. It looked like shaving cream was around their mouths, and the first thing I thought about was rabies. I didn't want to get bit by them, so I stomped my foot and ran at them as if I was on the attack.

They stopped, looked at each other, then stood on their hind legs, growling at me. That sent me running in the other direction. I wound up running all the way around the thirteenth floor until I came to apartment 13C. Once there, I beat on it while looking both ways.

Two older men who looked like they smoked heavy portions of crack cocaine turned the corner and came down the hall where I was standing. They had motor oil all over their clothes. I could see their hands were dirty, and their shoes were even worse. One of them, with a gray beard, looked me up and down and licked his lips. "Mm-hm. What do we have here?" he said, cupping his crotch.

His dark-skinned friend dug in his nose and moved his finger around before pulling it out and popping it over and over again. He looked me up and down as well, then smiled. "I don't know, but she better hope somebody answer that door."

I started to beat on the door faster and harder, praying Gino would open it soon. I was worried about being raped by one of those disgusting men. My heart started to skip a beat, and I felt like running if they got any closer. They were no more than fifty feet away and closing in.

Boom, boom, boom! "Gino! Gino! Open the door, ba-by. Please!" I hollered just as the door swung inward.

Gino snatched me in by my Chanel jacket with a scowl on his face. "Bitch, what the fuck you doin' beatin' on my door like you the muthafuckin' police? Huh?" he questioned with hate in his eyes.

His house smelled like onions and crack, as if somebody had been smoking the drug and cutting an onion at the same time. There were roaches crawling all over the floor, and he had a white pit bull whose ribcage was showing as if it never got fed.

I pointed to the men in the hallway. "Those old men were about to rape me. That's why I was beatin' on the door, baby. Calm down, please," I whimpered because I knew his temper was horrible.

He looked me over, then looked toward the hallway, taking a .357 revolver off of his waist and walking into the hallway. "Oh, is that right?" Once there, he raised the gun, I imagine at the men. "You bitch-ass niggaz trying to rape this girl in here? Huh?" he hollered, cocking the hammer on the weapon.

Though I couldn't hear them clearly, I imagined they were denying it, because Gino smiled and nodded his head up and down. "Yeah, I ain't think so. Let me ever catch any one of you niggaz fucking wit' a bitch that's in and out of my crib and it's gon' be a problem. Y'all got that?" He stepped into the house and slammed the door, making the dog jump up and run to the back of the house.

He locked the door, then looked me up and down. "What the fuck is you doing here? You better have something for me, or I'ma be forced to put one of these slugs in yo head. You know the homies back in Brooklyn got a hunnit bands on your life. I'm thinking about cashing you in, bitch. Word is bond." He sat down at the table, went into his pocket, and pulled out a glass pipe and a sandwich bag of rock cocaine. He broke a small piece off of it and stuffed the opening of his pipe with it before putting fire to the tip and inhaling deeply.

I was so scared my knees were knocking together. See, Gino was a well-known hit man from Brooklyn. I'd grown up with him, and we'd known each other ever since we were both five years old. Once upon a time we'd even had a relationship. Most recently I'd been getting together with him and giving whatever funds I could come up with. That always bought me a little more time. Usually after I paid him we'd fuck, and the deal would be sealed. To make matters even worse, I knew for a fact it was Gino's baby I was carrying simply because I'd already been pregnant by the time me and Sharome had first slept around.

I unzipped my Chanel jacket and pulled out my Chanel purse, reached inside, and took out the five thousand dollars I'd brought for him. I took a step forward so I could hand him the money. "Huh, Gino, this should buy me at least another week. By that time I'll have everything set up so you can get this nigga's whole safe I was telling you about. You'll make at least three hundred thousand dollars in cash, easy. Then we can focus on us," I said as he snatched the money from my hand.

He curled his upper lip as he counted the money in my face. "Five gees? Bitch, why you feeding me crumbs? If this nigga got three hundred gees put up, why you ain't bringin' me at least double digits?" he asked before slamming the money on the table. Then he turned back to me with his eyes bugged out of his head. They were glossy, and his breath smelled worse than a pig's ass. I wanted to throw up.

I was shaking like an amateur stripper. I knew Gino had a horrible temper. He never hesitated to kick my ass or knock a dude's head off. He had at least fifteen bodies under his belt. I knew that for a fact. He was not to be played with. "Gino, I have never steered you wrong, have I?" I stammered, ready to bust into a fit of tears.

The dog came back into the kitchen, sniffed my Steve Madden red-bottomed boots, and went on his way.

Gino laughed. "Bitch, you still alive, ain't you?" he smiled, then kicked the dog with all of his might right in the ribs. The dog flew upward and crashed into the refrigerator with a loud yelp before landing on its side, shaking with its eyes wide open.

I put my hands over my mouth in disbelief. Then Gino stepped forward and yanked my shirt upward, exposing my stomach. "You still got that punk-ass baby in there?" he asked, looking at me from the corner of his eye.

I took a step back, but it was of no use. He kept a firm hold on my shirt. "Yeah, but like I told you, you don't have to worry about it. This nigga thinks it's his baby, so I'm good for the rest of my life. He's a really good man. I almost hate setting him up like this, Gino."

Gino sucked his teeth and laughed. "What? Bitch, now all of a sudden you gettin' a conscience?" He slapped his thigh, laughing at the top of his lungs. "Ah-ha-ha. Ah, this dumb bitch said that."

Then he stopped and glared at me. I backed up with my hands in the air. "Gino, chill. I didn't mean it like that."

Gino upped his revolver and aimed it at my head, cocking the hammer once again, walking even closer to me until the cold steel was against my hot forehead. Then he grabbed me by the throat. "Bitch, you been layin' niggaz down wit' me ever since you was fourteen years old. You know how many niggaz in the grave because of that pussy between yo' legs? Huh?" he asked.

I nodded my head. "I do, Gino, and that's why I'm telling you I'ma handle bitness wit' him, too. I know what you need from me. I know you're the only reason I'm alive. I got this."

He turned the gun sideways and forced it into my skull even harder. "Bitch, you from Marcy Projects. You a hood bitch. You ain't never been shit, you ain't never gon' be shit. And the only reason you ain't stanking like a pile of shit is because I ain't pulled this trigger just yet. But it seem like you falling in love to me. Seem like you starting to care about this nigga. Is that the case? Huh, bitch?" He pushed me to the floor and kicked me in the side with his bare feet. His toenails were so long they cut me.

I scooted backward on my ass in sheer terror. "I don't care about nobody but you, Gino. Just you, baby. Fuck this nigga. We can do this shit tomorrow if you want to. Just say the word, Daddy," I whimpered with tears falling down my cheeks.

He looked down on me with a look of disgust. From my seat I could smell his feet. They smelled like corn chips and sugar.

He shook his head. "N'all, bitch. You see, I know what I gotta do for you. Sit yo' ass at that table and roll yo' sleeve back."

I shook my head side-to-side. "No, Gino, please. I'm begging you, not with the baby in me."

He exhaled through his nostrils. "Bitch, if I have to say it again, I'm blowing you and that punk-ass baby away. Get yo' ass up and do like I said. Now!" he hollered.

I damn near broke my neck getting to the table. I looked toward the kitchen and saw the dog was there hacking up big globs of blood. Every time he would cough, his ribs would go inward, then outward as the blood poured out of him. Finally, he lay on his side as big cockroaches crawled all over him.

I rolled back my sleeve as Gino came from the back room with a syringe and a small aluminum foil package of heroin. He sat across from me, took the heroin, and poured it inside a tablespoon. Then he took a drop of water and dripped it on top of the dope before lighting the bottom of it with a lighter. He allowed the dope to bubble up before he placed a piece of cotton on top of it, took the needle, and drew the liquid up into the syringe, turning toward me with a smile on his face.

"Give me your arm, bitch!"

I handed my right arm to him. He licked it, then began smacking it to make one of my veins pop up. I felt sick to my stomach. I was scared, and I didn't want the dope in my system. It had taken me nearly three years to kick it the first time. I survived by snorting methadone pills every now and then when the monkey came calling my name. Methadone and Oxy.

He took the needle and pierced my vein before injecting the fluid into me. As soon as the poison entered my system, it felt like I was having a massive orgasm. I squeezed my thighs together and moaned out loud. "Uh!"

He licked his crusty lips. "Yeah, that's the shit I'm talking about. Look at you now. This what you needed, ain't it, baby girl?"

I shook my head as my whole body went numb before the feeling of pleasure shot all over me. I felt happy. I felt free. I felt like only Gino could ever really understand me. I nodded my head. "It feels so good, Daddy. Damn. Fuck me right now! Hard. Please!" I begged, feeling my eyelids become too heavy for me to keep open.

Gino pulled me to the floor by my hair before straddling me. "Aw, don't worry, cuz from here on out it's gon' be in yo' system 'til that money sittin' in my lap. Daddy gon' be yo' pharmacist."

Chapter 9

Leesee

I sat there on the bed, feeling like there was a four-hundred pound sumo wrestler sitting on my chest. My ears were ringing, and my heart felt as if it was being ripped in two. Sharome stood in front of me in Tom Ford shorts and a black beater, his muscles popping on his frame, his black-and-white Yankees fitted cap turned to the back. On his waist were two chrome .44 Desert Eagles. I knew what kind they were because I'd asked him twice that day after forgetting the first time he'd told me.

It had been two months since I'd revealed to him I was pregnant with Savan's baby. My belly was protruding from my top. He paced back and forth in front of me, shaking his head as if he was about to lose his mind.

I rolled my head around on my neck again. "Rome, can you repeat that, please? My brain couldn't process everything. So, if you will, I'd really appreciate it. Don't leave anything out." I grabbed three tissues from the box of Kleenex, almost certain I would be crying soon. Ever since I found out I was pregnant it seemed my emotions were uncontrollable.

He took a deep breath and shook his arms out, then stopped a few feet away from me, looking me over. "Look, around the time you and that dude were doing your thing, and me and you were kind of distant toward one another, I turned to Tia since she was always under me and we were on the road together."

I blew out a gust of air and felt like I'd been gut-punched. Somewhere down deep in my soul I knew they'd been fucking around this whole time. I just felt it. I wanted to get up and attack his ass, but I wanted to hear it all. I didn't like there being so many secrets around me, so I rolled my head around on my shoulders and tried to maintain my composure.

He looked over to me and must've seen I was in distress. "You okay, baby?" He started to walk over to me.

I held up my hand. "I'm good, Sharome. Just finish telling me everything. And like I said before, don't leave nothin' out."

He swallowed and nodded his head, his chest muscles flexing. I reached and turned the fan, so the air was blowing directly on me, because it felt like my body's temperature had risen at least ten degrees. On top of that, I felt the baby moving inside of me. I had to pee again.

He cleared his throat. "A'ight, so anyway, just keepin' shit one real. I always thought Tia was fine, and her body did somethin' to me. I'm man enough to admit I was wrong for lustin' after your cousin, but I did. While you and Savan was getting' down, me and Tia was, too. Long story short, that baby she carrying in her belly is mine, and even though I still wanna work things out with you, I gotta be a man and take care of my responsibilities. I know I should've told you this, but I couldn't find the nerve. I ain't tryin' to lose you over this bullshit. I love you to death, A'Leeseea." His voice lowered at saying the last part.

I waddled my li'l pregnant ass out of the bed, walked up to him, and slapped the shit out of him as hard as I could. I hit his ass hard. He lowered his head and held his face, closin' his eyes. Then I saw his fist ball up. He looked down at me and raised it as if he was going to punch my lights out.

"That's my fuckin' cousin, Sharome! How could you? You tryin' to hurt me?" I screamed into his face, not caring if he hit me or not.

He bit into his bottom lip and flared his nostrils. "I know that, Leesee. Damn! What you want me to say? I fucked up. I only did that shit because I wasn't feelin' desired or needed by you. You started givin' me the cold shoulder, ma. Then she was there consolin' me, lettin' me know everything was gonna be alright, tellin' me how you needed me to get down in that bedroom so I could keep you. Then she just started showin' me some shit hands-on. I fucked up. We both did," he said, walking toward me and grabbing my hands.

I yanked my hands away from him and pushed him in the chest. "Don't touch me!" I screamed. He flew into the dresser, causing some of my hair care products to fall off of it. They crashed to the floor and busted open.

He caught his balance and jumped up, rushing me until he jacked me up against the wall by my shoulders. "Look, you putting your hands on me and shit ain't gon' fly. I told you what was good because I honestly am sorry. I wanna get past this after we figure this out on both sides. I'll do anything, A'Leeseea, damn!" He looked into my eyes, pleading.

I broke our eye contact and looked at the floor. "Sharome, you need to get your filthy hands off of me. You got me jammed up against this wall like I'm some punk bitch in the hood. You hollering you love me and shit, then let me down. Respect my reaction to all of this. As a man, accept that shit. You could have fucked anybody, Rome. Anybody. But you chose Tianna. My fuckin' blood."

The only sound in the room was coming from the whirring blades of the fan still aimed at the spot where I'd been sitting. Very slowly he released me and took four steps back. "You know what? You're right. Whatever you wanna do to me, I'm gon' give you the space to do it, 'cuz I was wrong. I should have never crossed that line with her. I should've had more respect for you and myself than I did." He held his arms out at his sides. "Do you, baby. Release that shit onto me."

I felt my heartbeat speed up. *Bam! Bam!* I swung twice with closed fists. The first blow caught him in the jaw, and the second in the nose, busting it. "That's my cousin, Sharome! My muthafuckin' cousin!" *Bam!* This blow caught him in the mouth, busting his lip.

He stumbled backward with blood dripping onto his beater. He shook his head, then took two steps forward and held his arms out in submission. "Come on, baby. I know you got more anger in you than that. You wanna hurt me? You wanna see me bleed? It's good. Come on, hurt me, baby. Hurt me, just so long as when you're done you'll still love me, because I need you more than anybody else in this world. You're my everything, and I'm sorry for hurtin' you, for crossin' you. I take full responsibility for my –"

Bam! Bam!

Two more hits, one to his jaw and the other to his massive chest. Then I was crying like a fuckin' baby because I'd made the man I loved more than my own self bleed with anger from my own hands. I ran to him and wrapped my arms around him.

He spat out blood before taking me in his arms. His chest heaved up and down. "I'm sorry, ma. All I can do is promise you I'll never hurt you like that again. I'ma raise this baby that's inside of you like it's my own. Y'all will never have to need for anything." He hugged me to him.

I felt the tears dripping off my chin. "Sharome, it hurts so bad. My heart feels like it's been torn in two, but I love yo' ass so much. Too fuckin' much."

He leaned to the side and spit a loogie of blood onto the floor. "I love you, too, and I swear I'm sorry. You're my everything. I'll never hurt you again."

Tia appeared, poking her head into the room with a smile on her face. Her eyes were low and glossy. "What you crazy kids in here doing?" she asked before stepping all the way in.

Before I could even think about it, I pushed Sharome away from me with so much force, sending him backward into the dresser, causing the mirror on top of it to fall forward and shatter across the floor. His gun had also fallen to the floor but thank God it didn't go off.

Tia's eyes got as big as paper plates. Before she could fully process I was coming at her, my fists were swinging wildly, catching her in the right eye, then the nose, and lastly the left eye before grabbing her hair and yanking her to the ground.

"Ah! What's wrong with this bitch? Ah! Getet her off me, Rome!" she hollered, trying to protect her face.

I wasn't having none of that. I punched her ass so much in the face that her head ricocheted off the floor repeatedly. "I. Trusted. You. Around. My. Man. Bitch! You. Got. The. Nerve. To. Get. Pregnant?" I screamed.

Sharome brought his strong ass over and yanked me off her. "Baby, it's not her fault. It's mine. I should have had more respect for you than I did."

I kicked my legs wildly. "Fuck that! She my cousin, and she didn't even tell me! What type of fuck-shit is that?" I hollered, trying to break free from his grasp.

Tia struggled to get up, blood pouring out of her nose. She held her stomach and used the door's handle to come to a stand.

I wiggled out of Sharome's hold and tackled her ass into the hallway, grabbing a handful of her hair and yanking her head backward. I had visions of punching her straight in the stomach with all the strength that I could muster, making her lose the baby that belonged to her and my first and only love. I couldn't stomach the thought of her giving birth to his seed. They would forever have a bond that would be unbreakable. I didn't know where that would leave me and Sharome, and it drove me loony.

Tia decided to finally fight back, slapping me across the face so hard I bit my tongue and fell off her and into the wall, dazed.

"Get off me, bitch!" she yelled, jumping up and grabbing my hair, pulling my head backward and causing my neck to pop.

"Uh! Uh! Let me go, you nasty hoe. Fight me head-up. Quit pulling on my hair and shit!" I hollered, smacking at her hands to try to free them. I wanted to kill this bitch. Not only was she fucking my man, but now she had the nerve to damn near knock me out. Oh, hell n'all, I wasn't going.

Sharome ran over and pried us apart. I waited until he got my hair free of her fingers, jumped up, and kicked her right in the gut. I got her ass good, too.

Tia let out a gust of air and flew backward into the living room before falling onto the glass table, shattering it. Glass flew into the air as it crashed inward.

"Leesee! What the fuck you just do, ma?" Sharome hollered, looking at me like I'd lost my mind.

I brushed past him and I was pretty sure he thought I was rushing to see if she was okay, but n'all, that was the furthest thing from my mind. I was about to really get all up in that ass. A smile crept upon my face as I watched her struggle to get up with glass shards all over her.

"Help me. It's glass cutting all into the back of my thighs," she groaned, slowly climbing out of the gold frame that had been holding the glass portion of the table.

Sharome attempted to run over to her, but I grabbed his arm. "Don't you fuckin' dare. This ain't got shit to do with you no more. It's between me and this bitch. We're blood, and she gotta answer for what she's done. That's just the way it is." I looked into his eyes and frowned.

Tia continued to climb out of the table's frame, glass crunching under her feet. She groaned with every step, looking as if she was about to faint.

Sharome looked her over with empathy. "Baby, you ain't got nothin' else to prove. Look at her. She fucked up. Let's just squash this shit and move on," he said, looking down into my eyes with his gray ones.

Tia came out of the frame, staggered, and fell on her ass. She got onto her knees and tried to come to a standstill again. It was then I saw the blood coming from a crack in her head. There was also a bunch coming from between her legs. She finally lay on her back with her legs up. "I wanted to tell you, Leesee," she said, out of breath. "Ask him. He told me not to." She placed her hand on her stomach and groaned loudly.

It took all of the discipline I had deep within me to not run over and stomp her ass out. I hated her with a passion.

I didn't give a fuck what she was saying, though it did make me look up to Sharome. "Is this true?" I growled.

Tia tried to get up again. "I need help. I'm bleeding between my legs. Help me, please," she whimpered.

Sharome nearly broke my heart when he brushed past me, ran over, and knelt beside her, helping her up. "I told her to wait for me to break the news to you, Leesee. I wanted to be a man and allow you to hear it from my mouth, not hers. So it's my fault," he convinced, walking her to the door.

Just seeing him hold her the way he was and knowing she had his baby inside of her was enough to make me irate all over again. "Ah! It doesn't fuckin' matter because both of y'all are bogus! Get yo' arm from around this bitch and let her drive herself to the hospital. Nigga, you belong to me. Point blank, period!" I screamed.

He shook his head. "Leesee, you are most definitely right about that. I do belong to you. But I gotta do what's right. If I don't get this girl to the hospital, not only could she lose the baby, but she could die. I can't have that on neither one of our consciences, because all it boils down to is we all made some terrible decisions that nobody should die over."

He opened the door after grabbing their coats and shoes, then left the house holding her up. The last sight of them caused me to fall to my knees and sob.

Chapter 10

Rome

Three days after the showdown between Tia and Leesee, I found myself sitting in our front room next to Leesee while Tia sat in the love seat with her head down. She'd just been released from the hospital less than two hours ago, and Leesee was still feeling some type of way. I was trying my best to play peacemaker.

Leesee rolled her head around on her shoulders. "Look, Tia, I'm glad you're okay and all that, but I still feel like hurtin' you. I don't know if it'll be smart for you to continue living here, because I don't know if I can control my temper. Every time I look at you now, all I see is a woman who betrayed me and is about to have my man's baby. It makes me sick to the stomach." She curled her upper lip.

Tia shrugged her shoulders in defeat. "So, what do you want me to do, Leesee? I ain't got no money to move out right now. I ain't got nowhere to go. Don't nobody care about me." She wiped tears from her face. "Y'all the only family I have," she sobbed.

I felt horrible. "Tia, you already know I'll make sure you're straight. You find a crib and I'll pay up your first six months of rent, and then keep checking in on you to make sure you're ahead on all of your bills. I ain't gon' let you go out like that because I'm at fault here, too," I said, feeling like a straight chump. I felt like Tia was getting the brunt of Leesee's wrath, and it wasn't fair. I was just as guilty, though I wished she would somehow just let it go. All of the dwelling was making our lives a living hell.

Besides, I wanted to address the heroin the doctors had found in Tia's system. I didn't think she knew that I knew, but after I let them know I was the father of the child she was carrying and her emergency contact person, the doctor had pulled me to the side and broke their doctor-patient confidentially clause. I needed to know if she was using, or had the drug made its way into her system just by handling it? I knew it was a possibility.

Leesee sucked her teeth. "You think I'm finna allow you to be walking around here, enticing him with yo' li'l chocolate ass? Shid, that's where I fucked up before, and look where it got me."

Tia looked over to her and frowned. "N'all, that ain't what got you in trouble, Leesee. Let's not forget you was too busy fuckin' some older dude because Sharome couldn't get you right. You blamin' all of this shit on us and ain't assumin' none of the responsibility. Go figure." She rolled her eyes and lowered her head again.

Leesee bounced her feet up and down on her toes as she sat beside me, looking like she was ready to attack Tia once again. For Tia's sake, it was best she pipe down. "Bitch, what the fuck my business got ta do with you? You shoulda keep yo legs closed. What I was doin' didn't give you the right to my man. Period! You scandalous, skank ass hoe ! Bitch, you gon' have me do somethin' to yo' ass you wouldn't be able to recover from. Stop fuckin' playin' with me, TIANNA."

Tia looked up at her. "A'Leeseea, if I didn't have this baby in me, I would fuck you up. I ain't scared of you. I'm from Brooklyn, bitch. I grew up fightin' every day of my life. Don't get it twisted." She sucked her teeth. "I just ain't tryna lose *our* baby."

96

Leesee jumped up and threw the coffee table that separated us from Tia, out the way. "Well, lucky for me, I don't give a fuck whether I lose my baby or not, so what's good?"

She made a move to attack her, and Tia jumped up and ran behind her loveseat. "Sharome, you better get this crazy bitch. I ain't goin' back to the hospital for fightin' her."

I got up and pulled Leesee into my embrace. "Chill, ma. Let's talk about this like civilized adults. Ain't no reason to keep fightin'. I'm with you forever, ma. You hear me?"

She mugged Tia with hatred for a long time before looking up at me. "I ain't tryna hear that shit, Rome. You better get an understanding with this bitch, because I'm done. And matter o' fact, I tell you what. You can have this house, Tia. We'll move. I don't want to be reminded every single day of what took place here. So I'll go out and find a new crib for us." She shook her head, went into our bedroom, and came back out with her clutch and car keys before putting a pair of pink and black Airmax 95s on her feet. "I need some fresh air. I'll be back, Sharome. Try not to fuck this bitch again while I'm gone." She mugged us both, before she left the house.

Tia waited for the sound of Leesee's ignition to turn over before she stood up with tears running down her cheeks. "How dare you let her treat me like that, Rome? I'm the mother of your child. I don't give a fuck what y'all had goin' on before I came into the picture. I'm here now, and I am pregnant with your kid. You have to honor me more than you do. You know how much I love you!" she hollered, running over to me and wrapping her arms around my waist, laying her head on my chest.

I held her for a second, then broke our embrace. "Man, I care about you, too, but that's my woman. I'll die for her. She has to be my first and foremost from here on out. As much as I know you hate hearin' that, it's the truth," I said, feeling beads of sweat come onto my forehead.

Tia took a step back and looked up at me with anger on her face. "What's so good about her, Sharome? Huh? Y'all wasn't together that long before she cheated on you. She started fucking with another man as soon as y'all left Jersey, and that's even with you saving her life. But none of that mattered to her. She's walking around with another man's baby. What part of that don't you understand, dummy?" She shook her head and kissed her teeth. "Here I am carrying your first and only child. I've been faithful to you since day one even though you've kept me on the sidelines, in need of you more often than not. I've been with you when others have tried to kill us. I've been your rider. But what do I get for all of that? Nothing!" She turned her back to me and placed her hands over her face, crying into them.

I lowered my head and exhaled loudly. Once again, I was feeling like I was making a wrong decision. Everything Tia was saying to me was the truth. She was having my first child. She had been real with me ever since we'd met. She'd faced the barrel of a gun beside me when our lives were on the line, and ever since she came into the picture she'd been my rider, even in times when Leesee had not been. The truth sucked, and it made me feel some type of way for her all over again.

I walked to her back and turned her around, pulling her into my embrace and hugging her. "Tia, everything you sayin' is the truth. I don't want you to feel like I don't acknowledge and honor everything you've done, because I do. I love you for all of them, and I owe you more love than I've been giving to you." I exhaled again. "This shit is so hard because I love Leesee so fuckin' much, to the point I will die for her in a heartbeat. She is my everything, but at the same time I can't get you off my heart, either. I hate feeling like I'm doing you wrong. I wish there was a way where we could all be happy, but it ain't. So, as a man, I have to do what's right, and that's make sure you're well taken care of, along with our child. She saying you can keep this crib. Well, I'm thinking we go and cop you a place better than this one. I want you to have the best of the best because that's what you deserve. Don't think that just because I'm with Leesee I ain't gon' keep you up to par. I'm more of a man than that."

Tia broke out of my embrace and pushed me backward. "I don't care about your fuckin' money, Sharome. I care about you. That bitch care about what's in your safe. I don't. I'd be with you if you were broke and living on the streets." She wiped her tears away, shook her head, then wrapped her arms around herself as if she was cold. "I feel sick. I need a minute." She walked away from me and headed up the stairs to her apartment.

I grabbed her arm and pulled her to me. "You usin' that shit, Tia? Huh?" I asked, looking her over.

Her eyes were wide, tear streaks all over her cheeks. She shook her head, then yanked her arm away, walking backward. "Yeah, Rome, I am, because you're taking me through so much. My only escape is to report back to what I was used to back in the day. So yeah, I'm using heroin. What you gonna do about it?" she asked, challenging me.

I felt my heart pounding in my chest as I looked her over with anger rising within me. I didn't understand how a person could be so stupid, so careless. I wondered how much of an affect her drug use was going to have on our child. I stepped forward until I was directly in her face. "You pregnant with my kid, and yet you decide it's in your best interest to kill him or her by using that poison?"

She shrugged her shoulders. "And? You don't give a fuck about me, so why do you ask?" She laughed. "I know you were hoping I'd lose this baby, Rome. You hate that I'm pregnant. You wish Leesee was carrying this baby, and I was carrying the one she has. Admit it. I wanna hear you say it," she demanded, tears running down her cheeks again.

I grabbed her shoulders and shook her a bit. "Stop saying that dumb shit. Why you usin' this poison? Who givin' you this shit? Is it anybody from Harlem? One of my niggaz?" I asked, ready to bust a muthafucka's head over this.

She yanked her arm away and made her way up the stairs again. "Fuck you, nigga. I'm gon' do what I wanna do until you tell me I'm your number one. I love you too much to not be with you, Rome. I can't take this shit you puttin' me through. I just can't. You're killin' me, and you don't even know it." She jogged all the way up the stairs, got to the top, and looked down on me. "I'll be out of here in a week. I won't need your help once I leave. I don't need nobody!" she screamed and slammed her upstairs door.

I wanted to run up there, break the door down, and kiss her or kick her ass for using that shit, but I knew it wouldn't solve anything. I felt powerless in the situation. She was not my woman. Had it been Leesee, I would have snapped out and turned all the way up, forcing her into rehab or something. Though she was pregnant with my kid, I still didn't feel like it was my place to control her, so I let it be just as my phone rang.

About four hours later, and just as the sun was setting, Ramsey pulled up in a Bentley truck, blowing the horn just as I was closing the door behind me. I'd left Leesee in the bedroom where she'd taken an Advil PM because she's caught one of her more serious migraines. Tia had not come down the stairs ever since she'd went up them hours ago.

When I got into the truck, Ramsey handed me two Ziplocs full of hundred dollar bills. "That's you, li'l homie. That's a hundred bands right there. I want you to bust this move with me tonight and bust one of my li'l niggaz' head. Then I'ma put you in his slot. He been coming up short on my scratch, skimming off the top and plotting against me with a few niggaz from the Bronx. Niggaz don't trust kid like that, so word got back to me immediately. We gotta exterminate this rat right away so our operation don't crumble. Nah mean?" He sipped out of his pink Sprite before twisting the cap back on it.

I turned the Ziploc bags over in my hands and smiled. "I'm surprised you won't have one of yo' hittas knock him off."

Ramsey pulled away from the curb and shook his head. "N'all, that'd be too easy. You see, I want this nigga to suffer and look into the eyes of the man that's gon' take his slot once we bury him." He curled his lip and frowned. "I don't fuck with no snakes, Sharome. I hate 'em. I make sure every nigga on my team eat good. Ain't nobody starving because whenever I eat, y'all eat.

101

That's the way it's always been. I'm a real Blood nigga. That shit runs through my veins, kid."

He circled around my block and pulled right back to the front of my house. I looked up at it, then at him. "What's good? Why we back here?"

He pointed at my lap. "Li'l homie, go put yo' money up. I just told you we finna go and whack a nigga. You don't need to walk around wit' a hundred thousand to do that," he laughed and sat back in his seat.

I jumped out of the truck and ran up the stairs and into the house just as Tia was walking into the kitchen with a dirty plate in her hand. When she saw what I was carrying, her eyes got big. She licked her lips.

I stopped and busted one of the Ziplocs open. "Look, I don't know how much of a hold that dope got on you, but here." I pulled out about fifteen grand and gave it to her.

She took it and wiped her mouth. "What is this for?"

I shook my head. "For nothing. I love you, girl, and I swear I'ma make sure you're always taken care of."

Ramsey blew his horn twice. I jogged down the hallway and opened our bedroom door just as Leesee was coming out of the bathroom with her stomach exposed and poking out. "Baby, look, this eighty-five thousand dollars. I need you to put it in the safe for me. I gotta go," I said, running up to her and kissing her on the cheek.

She took the money and looked me over as if I was crazy. "Wait, baby, what's the code," she yelled as I made my way down the hallway.

"It's your date of birth. I thought I told you that already," I yelled, opening the front door.

Tia waved to me from the kitchen. "Be careful out there, Sharome. I love you," she whispered.

I looked down at her stomach, saw the bulge, and closed the door after telling her I would be.

Jelissa

Chapter 11

Leesee

I knelt down and moved all of Sharome's Jordan and Timberland boxes out of the way before pulling the loose piece of wall outward and placing it to the side. Once it was out of the way, I pulled his digital safe out and opened the panel so I could punch in the code, but before I could I felt a presence behind me. It caused the hair to stand up on the back of my neck. I turned around and nearly jumped out of my skin as I saw Tia standing over me.

"Holy fuck! Tia, what are you doing in my room?" I hollered, pushing Sharome's safe back into the wall and standing up.

She backed up, holding her hands in the air. One of them was filled with a few stacks of money. "Look, I'm not trying to get no bullshit started with you. Sharome just came in and gave me this fifteen thousand dollars. I don't know if he told you about it, but I just wanted to let you know because I no longer want to do anything behind your back," she said in a calm manner.

I looked her up and down. "That's how much?" I asked, feeling some type of way. Even though to Sharome that wasn't much money, to a bitch who didn't have shit, that was a lot. I felt jealous.

"It's fifteen thousand. I'll give it to you if you want me to, but he said it was mine." She held it out to me.

I almost grabbed it away from her but decided against it. I wanted to go another route. "Nah, that's yours. He probably know you gon' need that li'l paper down the road when we leave from here, 'cause it won't be long.

Besides, he gave me this to put up for *us*." I made sure I put a strong emphasis on the word 'us,' then grabbed the two Ziploc bags of money and held them in her face.

It looked like her entire soul escaped from her body. She turned a shade lighter. "Oh, damn. How much is that?" she asked, sounding like she was ready to cry.

I laughed and knelt down, pulling his safe out of the closet. "It's eighty-five gees. Just a li'l chump change. I'm used to seeing him bring this type of shit home." I punched in the code on the digital keypad and it popped open. I made sure I sat to the side so Tia could see all of the rows and rows of cash inside. Very slowly I started to unload the Ziploc bags of money, placing them into the safe that looked like a mini refrigerator.

She gasped, and it made me smile.

"Yeah, that's why I say you can keep this house, because I want something better than this rat hole. I mean, it's nice, but I deserve somethin' better. I am a queen. He tell me that all the time." I smiled even harder and looked over my shoulder at her. "How much money you got put up altogether?" I asked, curious.

I knew Sharome had a thing for giving me frivolous amounts of cash, and I wondered if he made it a point to do the same thing for her. If he had, I was going to bust his head when he got home.

She shrugged her shoulders. "Well, this fifteen, and I got about three gees upstairs." She sounded defeated. "Why, how much do you have? Or is all of y'all's money put together for the both of y'all to spend?" She scratched her arm, then started to rub it.

I stuffed a bundle of cash into his safe, then dug back into the Ziploc bag for another one. I was happy she kept on setting me up to shit on her ass. In my mind I felt like I needed to make her feel as low as possible so she could see Sharome cared about me way too much to ever take whatever they had going on behind my back seriously. She needed to know I was his one and only, and she was just recreational fun.

I shook my head. "N'all, we spend this money from his safe, but I also got my own safe, and we never touch the money out of it because Sharome says it belongs to me, and I am to do whatever with it I want to. He says we will never spend my money, that for as long as he's out there hustling and bringing home bundles of cash, all I needed to do is stack my paper up just in case something ever happened to him." I sighed. "That's my baby. He loves me so much."

I looked over my shoulder at her to see her stupid-ass face. She had her lip poked out like a little kid, looking at the fifteen thousand dollars in her hand as if it was nothing more than a few peanuts. Her facial expression was priceless. "Dang. Well, how much money do you got put up for a rainy day?"

I closed Rome's safe and pushed it back into the wall, fitting the piece in place before putting his shoeboxes the way they were, then closing the closet door. I reached to the ground and grabbed the Ziploc bag I had purposely kept about forty thousand dollars in. I took it, walked over to the dresser, and moved it just enough so I could get to my mini safe. I wanted to flex on this bitch. I knew she was able to calculate about how much money was in Rome's safe. It had to be every bit of five hundred thousand dollars. I wanted to show her the two hundred thousand I had, and not to mention the forty I'd just taken.

I moved the dresser away from the wall enough so I could remove the back of it. Once I did, I pulled out my safe that weighed about seven pounds before the money was added to it. I looked over to Tia and smiled as I popped it open.

She took a step to the right and looked over my shoulder and into it with her eyes big as paper plates. "Damn, all that's yours?" she asked in amazement, giving me the response I was looking for.

I giggled. "Yeah, it's about two hundred and forty thousand after I add this li'l chump change to it. This what I got in cash. I got another hundred in my Chase account, too. Life is good when your man really loves you." I looked up at her and laughed.

She lowered her head and shook it. "Damn, and here I was thinking I was doing something. I see he don't really love me like he do you. I feel so stupid, but that's what I get, though. It is what it is." She exhaled loudly, looked down at the money in her hand, and started to walk out of the room.

I bounced to my feet and cut her off, stepping into her face. "Wait a minute, Tia. Explain that last comment, because you just fucked me up with that one," I said, feeling my temper getting hot. I was really starting to hate this bitch, blood or not.

Tia flared her nostrils and placed her hand on her stomach just like she always did when her and I got into a confrontation or argument. I think it was her way of reminding me she was pregnant and I should somehow take pity on her, but it never worked. It always made me want to fuck her up even more.

"Look, Leesee, I didn't mean nothing by it. I was really talking to myself more than anything. Just forget I even said somethin."

I shook my head and blocked her path again as she tried to step around me. I didn't like when a person dismissed me or didn't answer the questions I asked them. It made me feel insulted, especially when it came to finding things out about her and Sharome. I wasn't wit' that shit. "N'all, you need to let me know what the fuck you thought was going to happen between you two? Did you think that just because y'all were fucking and you got pregnant that you was gon' be able to take him away from me or something? Huh?" I asked, curling my upper lip and looking this bitch in her eyes.

She stared at me for a long time, before smacking her lips, and bumping past me. "I ain't got time for this shit tonight. I need to figure my life out, because obviously yours is set."

I stood there with steam coming off of my head as she walked down the hallway and into the kitchen. I had visions of running in there, opening one of the drawers, grabbing a knife, and cuttin' her ass into shreds. I was tired of this bitch being in our house. I was tired of her being around Sharome. I was tired of knowing she was pregnant by him and forcing myself to imagine what it was going to be like having her and this new-ass baby in our lives for the next eighteen-plus years. I was over it.

I ran my hand over my face, and exhaled, walking into the kitchen with bullshit on my mind. She was standing in the door of the refrigerator, drinking out of the Minute Maid orange juice container. I walked right up to her and smacked it out of her hands just as her lips were going in for another swallow. The juice spilled all over her face and white t-shirt, and I didn't give no fucks. She inhaled loudly as if she was about to drown. She jumped back as the container fell on the floor and kept on oozing juice.

"What the fuck is your problem, Leesee?" she screamed with a frown on her face, looking down at her drenched shirt and short shorts.

I walked over to the drawer of knives and pulled out a big steak one, slammed the drawer back, walked over to her, and slammed the knife down on the counter in front of her. I glared into her eyes with hatred as I felt my ears ringing and sweat pouring down my forehead because I was so heated. "Bitch, I asked you a fucking question, and you gon' answer my question. I need to know what the fuck you thought was going to happen between you and Sharome, and I need to know right the fuck now!" I hollered and picked the knife back up, pointing the blade toward her.

She backed into the refrigerator, stepping into the puddle of juice with her bare feet. The liquid crept through the small cracks between each of her toes. "Leesee, get off of that bullshit. I told you I was just talking out loud." She swallowed and bugged her eyes out of her head.

I stepped forward into the puddle of juice and put the blade to her throat. At that time, I didn't know if I was going to cut her or not, but I was definitely on the verge. I was tired of playing with this broad. I needed to know if she targeted Sharome like most project girls did whenever they saw or heard about a good man being around. I knew she had some shysty shit in her character, but I guessed I was too blind to see it when me and Sharome were first leaving Jersey, though I could tell she was feeling him on some lustful shit. But that was a given because he was so damn fine, with those gray eyes and all. "Tell me the truth!"

She blinked tears. "Okay, okay, damn. Calm the fuck down, it's not that serious." She backed further into the refrigerator as I scrunched my face and put the blade on her neck. She swallowed. "I guess I thought once he found out I was pregnant he would care about me at least as much as he does you, if not more." Tears dropped off her chin. "I don't know why I was thinking like that, but I was. I'm just being honest," she said, looking at the blade from the corner of her eye.

I had visions of slicing her throat once again. I felt my brain begging me to do it, telling me she deserved to die for fucking with my man behind my back. I clenched my teeth together and held it steady against her throat. "Did you target him from the get-go, or did you fall for him all of the sudden? And don't lie to me, Tia, because you best believe I already know what's good. I just wanna hear the truth out of your mouth."

She tilted her head back, shaking it as tears ran out of her eyes. "N'all, it wasn't nothin' like that. I fell for Sharome over time because he is such a great guy. I've never seen any man treat a woman like he treated you. Even though he's a street nigga, he treats you like a princess, and I wanted some of that for myself. But I didn't target him off the rip. My urge for him sorta developed on its own. I can't help the way I feel. I wish I could," she whimpered, keeping her face tilted toward the ceiling.

I held the knife to her throat for about a minute longer, then pushed her back into the refrigerator. It rocked and two boxes of Captain Crunch Berries fell from it and onto the floor. "Tia, you know what? You ain't even worth it. I want you to get your shit together and be out of here in less than a week. I don't want you around Sharome no more, especially if I ain't present. If I catch you sniffing around my man, bitch, on my mama, I'm gon' kill you and spend the rest of my life in prison."

Tia started to cry harder. "I don't know where to go, Leesee. I ain't got nobody. I ain't got all of that money put up like you do. I wish I did. So where am I supposed to go?"

I placed the knife in the sink and turned around to face her. "I don't give a fuck where you go, but you gon' get the fuck out of here. That's for damn sure. Whatever place you find, like he said, we'll pay up your rent and get you ahead, but this me, you, and Sharome relationship is over. He belongs to me and only me. Forever. Deal wit' it."

Tia was silent for a long time, then she began nodding her head up and down, looking me over closely. "A'right, Leesee. Okay. If that's how you want it, I got you."

Chapter 12

Rome

I felt the sweat drip down my back and my bulletproof vest sticking to me. My flesh crawled as I watched the fifty-plus rats feed on the two dead bodies on the floor in the corner of the boiler room. They smelled like boiled cats and burnt tires. I tried my best to breathe through my mouth, but it only made me feel sick. The air was so thick I could literally taste the poison the wafted through the air.

Ramsey walked up to the heavyset, light-skinned man and stuffed another peanut butter sandwich into his mouth, putting a pistol to his forehead. "Chew up, bitch-nigga, or I'm knocking your head off your shoulders right here and right now," he growled.

The man chewed with his eyes wide open. "Ramsey, this shit ain't right, my nigga." More chewing. He sounded out of breath. "All that shit them niggaz feeding you is bullshit." More chewing. "I would never play wit' yo' paper." He stuck his head forward and struggled to swallow the fifth peanut butter sandwich Ramsey had forced him to eat.

Ramsey laughed, turned around, and walked over to the table, grabbing the peanut butter off of it. He took a huge glob and forced it into the man's mouth. The man tried to yank his head away, then Ramsey smacked him with his .9 millimeter so hard that it sounded like he broke something in his jaw.

"Argh! What the fuck, nigga!" he hollered, spitting blood and peanut butter out on the floor.

Ramsey grabbed him by his long dreads and spit into his face. "Bitch-ass nigga, I been personally keepin' yo' books and logging every transaction you've made ever since I put you in power. You been fucking me over since day one. Ain't no loyalty nowhere in you." He scrunched his face and looked over his shoulders at me. "Lil homie, you ready to body this nigga so I can put you in his slot?" he asked with a smile on his face.

I nodded my head. "Hell yeah, I got his bitch-ass. You say since he lied to you, you want his tongue out, right?" I asked, moving the tools around in the toolbox until I found the vice grips. Once I found them, I walked over to Ramsey as he stepped away from the light-skinned stud.

Ramsey pulled out a blunt so fat it looked like a brown Twinkie. He put fire to the tip and inhaled the smoke deep into his lungs. "Hell yeah. Y'all come over here and hold this nigga head while my li'l nigga do his thing," Ramsey ordered his hittas, who were standing guard all over the boiler room of the projects.

Two of the heavier-set ones jogged over and held the yellow dude's head, forcing his mouth open for me. I felt all sorts of anxieties as I stepped forward and placed the vice grips in his mouth as he struggled to yank his head away, hollering at the top of his lungs. His breath smelled like peanut butter and shit. "Argh, on't oo ee ike dis!" he hollered, not able to pronounce his words because his mouth was being held wide open.

I slid the vice grips inside his mouth and locked them on his tongue before pulling backward with all of my might. I closed my eyes as I saw how his tongue was being stretched all weird-like. I couldn't lie and say it didn't freak me out, but I had to make a statement in front of Ramsey and his surrounding crew. The new position I was about to receive would ensure I would make no less than fifty gees a week. With two babies on the way and always trying to stay ahead on the bills, the money was greatly needed. I couldn't fail Leesee. I had to make sure Tia never needed for anything, no matter if her and I were together or not. She was now my full responsibility. I owed her a life of stability.

"Argh! Argh!" The yellow man started to jerk in the chair he was duct taped to. Sweat poured down his forehead. His eyes were so wide they looked like they were about to pop out of his head.

I opened my eyes and pulled backward, taking his tongue as far out of his mouth as his muscle would allow. It looked like a thick piece of bubble gum. I clenched my teeth and kept on pulling.

Ramsey appeared beside me with a pair of gardening shears. "This is what a muthafucka get when they tell a bold-face lie right to my face. Bitch-nigga, I'm Capo!" He placed the yellow man's tongue between the gardening shears as I pulled it even further out of his mouth. Then he snipped it and cut it completely off.

"Argh!" he hollered.

I staggered backward and nearly busted my shit before I caught my balance. Looking down at the vice grips as he screamed his head off, I saw the half of his tongue that was no longer attached to the rest of him. I bugged my eyes out of my head and felt like I wanted to puke. I had never seen no shit like that before, but apparently Ramsey and his goons had because they were laughing and cheering the act on as if it was a part of some television series.

"Hell yeah! That's how you do that shit, Sharome. Now do his eyes so we can throw his punk-ass in the corner with the rest of them fuck-niggaz that the hood dismissed." He handed me a flat-head screwdriver.

The yellow man had blood pouring out of his mouth as if he was throwing up cherry Kool-Aid. It ran down his neck and into his lap. He shook as if he was having a seizure. I could smell he'd also released his bowels. The scent breezed through the air, adding to those of the dead bodies over in the corner.

I walked up to the yellow man with my heart pounding in my chest. I felt a little dizzy, and everything seemed surreal. I had to overcome this last step, and then I would have the fifty-thousand-a-week gig in Ramsey's crew. I wouldn't have to do nothing but check on trap houses and collect the money, bring it back to him, and occasionally travel out of town so I could meet with other kingpins. It would be so simple. At eighteen I would be vastly ahead of the game, able to provide like never before.

"Get his ass, Sharome. Handle that bidness, li'l homie, then let's go and celebrate Harlem-style. Word is bond!"

I was in no position to think about it. I took a deep breath, walked up to the yellow man, and clenched my teeth after dropping the vice grips with his tongue to the floor. I exhaled loudly, reached back, and then jammed the screwdriver forward with all of my might into his left eye, hearing it pop loudly as it entered, getting caught.

"Ah!" he screamed, sounding like a female. He legs, which were duct taped together, suddenly broke the tape and kicked into the air wildly.

I pulled the screwdriver back out with his eyes attached to it for a second, then it snapped off of the end and fell against his cheek, hanging on by the long tendon that was still in his socket.

"Hell-muthafucking-yeah!" Ramsey hollered. "That's for being so fuckin' greedy, my nigga. You saw what I had, and you wanted. Give me that muthafucka, Sharome. I'll take it from here." He grabbed the screwdriver from me and jammed it into the man's other eye while he screamed at the top of his lungs. He chastised him the entire way, letting him know why it all was happening to him.

I stood wit' my back against the wall, watching the event play out. I felt like I was having an out-of-body experience. I couldn't believe what had taken place, couldn't believe I had actually been a part of it.

Ramsey continued to go to work on the yellow man until his chair fell backward, stomping his head into the concrete while his goons looked on, along with me. Part of me felt like I was entering into a part of the game that was too deep for me, but another part knew I could handle it.

Later that night, Ramsey threw a party in my honor to announce my new status to the rest of his crew. The party was at a nice mansion out in the Hamptons. By the time we got done getting rid of the bodies in the boiler room, it was one in the morning. For the most part I was exhausted, but Ramsey insisted I shower, which I did in the projects. Then he gave me a fresh red-and-black Gucci fit that I slipped into and capped off with the red-and-black retro number eight Jordans. I put a Chicago Bulls cap on my deep waves and turned it to the back.

By the time we got to the mansion, the party was already in full swing. I walked through the door and was met with the flashing lights of the party. Ramsey wrapped his arm around my neck as he turned up a bottle of Ace of Spades. "Nigga, this the life you finna live right here, kid.

All these muthafuckas here to celebrate the new you, your newfound success with the mob, my nigga. I told you I was gon' make sure you ate." He hugged me tighter, then let me go as two thick-ass caramel sistas walked up wearing just their bras and panties. The fronts of their panties were all up in their lips. I can't even lie and say my piece didn't stir in my boxers, because it did.

Ramsey leaned his face forward as both chicks kissed him on each cheek while *Bank Account* by 21 Savage banged out of the speakers of the party. "Yo! This my li'l nigga Sharome, right here! He taking over for Dexter. He's my general. Treat him like a muthafucking king every time you see him and you ain't never gotta worry about yo' bills being paid. That's on my blood. You hoez get that?" he hollered because the music was so loud.

They looked me over with hunger in their eyes while they nodded their heads. The one wearing an all-red bra and panty set stepped up to me and kissed me on the lips, sucking on them before I pushed her back. "Hold on, li'l mama, this ain't that type of party. I got a wife at home," I said, even though my dick was standing straight up, ready for action.

Ramsey waved me off. "Shid, I do, too, but that ain't never stopped a boss from having fun." He laughed and turned the bottle of champagne back up as the other chick fell to her knees and started to rub the front of my Gucci pants. She squeezed my dick through them and unzipped my zipper, reaching her hand inside and pulling my piece out, licking the head.

I must've let her lick me five times before I jumped back and put my dick back up. Ramsey was already getting his dick sucked by the other one with his eyes closed. He humped into her mouth again and again while the other one looked up at me with hunger in her eyes.

"Come on, Daddy. Let me show you how us Blood Queens get down. I promise you once I wrap my lips around that big muthafucka, you gon' forget all about yo' wife. I stand on that." She reached and grabbed my dick again.

I shook my head and slapped her hand away. As much as I wanted to, I couldn't betray Leesee like that again. I'd given her my word. It was bad enough I'd allowed her to lick my shit five times without pushing her ass away. That was as far as I was willing to go. "I'm good, ma. Maybe I'll catch you on the rebound," I said, zipping up.

She shrugged her shoulder, then scooted over to Ramsey along with her friend. They took turns sucking homie off until he came over both of their faces.

About twenty minutes later and after he washed up, he led me to the back room where I shook up with a few of his top goons. We got an understanding amongst each other before we headed back out into the party. As soon as I got on the dance floor, I was surrounded by some of the baddest women I had ever seen in my life. They danced all over me and rubbed up and down my chest and stomach muscles, kissing all over my neck, squeezing my dick, and whispering in my ear a lot of kinky shit that had my mind wondering. I kept seeing Leesee's face and thinking them broads was going to make it hard for me, but I had to do my best to hold her down.

While I danced on the floor, I drank out of a bottle of Ace of Spades and smoked a blunt as fat as a Twinkie that Ramsey had given me. I felt like a boss and figured if every day felt like that night felt, then I was ready to be Ramsey's general. I would just have to get my discipline together when it came to all of the beautiful and willing women who were sure to be around me at all times.

Before Ramsey dropped me off that night, he hugged me. "Look, Sharome, all I ask is for your loyalty. Never let the money get the best of you. This game is cold, and it's cutthroat. Remember, the most important hand is the one that feeds you. Blood in, my li'l nigga, Blood out."

Chapter 13

Tia

I felt my whole body shaking as I waited for Gino to sit down and pick up the phone on the other side of the glass. I didn't know what he was about to say to me, but I sincerely hoped he would hear me out. I only needed a little more time.

It had been three days since Leesee had told me I had to be out of her house. Three days and I'd still not found a new place to go. In the mornings when we crossed paths, she'd give me the stink-eye, looking me up and down before reminding me how many days I had left until it was time to get the hell out of her crib.

I saw movement in front of me. Seconds later Gino was being seated on the other side of the county jail's protective glass. He scrunched his face, took the phone, and wiped it on his shirt before placing it to his ear. He knocked on the glass and pointed at the one I was supposed to be talking into. I hurriedly picked it up as I felt my baby kicking inside of my stomach. The feeling of needing to pee nagging at me.

He exhaled loudly and wiped his mouth with his hand. "Tia, why the fuck am I still sitting in this punk-ass jail? Why the fuck you ain't paid that li'l bail?" he snapped into the phone, looking me in the eyes.

My whole body was shaking worse than before. "I didn't even know you had a bail, Gino, so please calm down and just tell me how much it is. I'll figure it out," I said as calm as I possibly could. I didn't want to get into an argument with him. I knew his temper was horrible, and he was very irrational.

He flared his nostrils, looked up at the ceiling, and shook his head. "I went to by bail hearing this morning. All I need is ten gees and they gon' let me up out of here. It's a simple possession charge, no biggie. That mutha-fucking bill so high because it's my third one in two months. I gotta get up out of here, though. I got warrants all over the east coast. I'm trying to be up out this bitch before they discover all that. You understand what I'm saying?" he asked, scratching his neck.

I nodded my head and smiled. "I got you, baby. You know I do. I'll handle this bidness ASAP. Soon as I leave here I'm going to get a bail bondsman, have him do that shit electronically."

He nodded and shrugged his shoulders as if something was crawlin' all over him. "I'm sick in this bitch. Make sure you have some dog food for me as soon as I come through that door. I feel like my insides being ripped out of me." He wrapped his arms around his body. "What's good with that other move?"

I moved around uncomfortably in my seat. "Baby, it's good. I think once you get out and you rest up for a few days, we hit their ass. It's a guarantee we'll walk away with no less than three hundred thousand. I just found out my cousin has a safe, too, with about two hundred thousand in it. I wanna hit her at the same time we hit her man. Fuck both of them. It's all about you and I. I wanna see you shine like back in the day. You remember when you had the money-green Porsche?" I asked, smiling and thinking back to the days when Gino was a straight baller and moved heroin by the kilo all over New York.

He nodded and laughed a little. "Yeah, it's about time I get back on my throne. I always knew it was going to be you that got me there. You've always been my bottom bitch, even when we weren't together."

I didn't know if I liked him calling me a bitch. It made me feel lower than scum, but I knew it was in my best interest to play the role he needed me to because this man literally had my life in the palms of his hands. Had it not been for him, I was sure my enemies out of Marcy Projects would have tracked me down and finished me in the streets. There were so many rumors floating around Brooklyn that I was responsible for setting up a few hustlers to be robbed and killed – rumors that were honestly the truth. My old sins were coming back to haunt me, and Gino said the hustlers of Brooklyn had come together to place a hundred thousand dollar bounty on my head. It was enough to give me nightmares every single night, without fail.

I smiled at Gino. "Well, at least you know, though. That's all that matters to me."

He fidgeted in his seat and dug into his ear, looking at his finger with a crazy look on his face. "How is our baby doing?"

I nearly fell out of the seat at hearing him say that. I felt my blood pressure rise and everything. "He's good, baby. I'm surprised to hear you call him ours. It warms my heart," I said, feeling emotional.

He wiped earwax on his pants legs, then tried to rub it off with his hand. "Yo, once you get me out of here, I promise you gon' see a whole new me. This muthafucka make you think harder than you ever have before. I know I gotta do right by you, if not nobody else. You my baby. So when I touch down, we gon' chill for a few days, then we gon' hit that lick and get the fuck out of New York. Word is bond. I'm thinking rolling out to Houston or somethin', fucking wit' my sister out that way. What you think?" he asked, licking his dry lips.

I shrugged my shoulders. "Baby, to be honest, I'll go wherever you want to go. Long as you let me have your back, I'll be right by your side, riding like I'm supposed to be." I felt the baby kick me again. I had to pee so bad it hurt.

Gino ran his tongue across his teeth. "Yeah, I bet. Well, you just get me up out of here, and we'll go from there. I ain't trying to spend more than another day. Handle yo' bidness, or I'ma get out of here on my own and fuck you. You got that?"

He dropped the phone, mugged me through the glass, then turned his back on me and started to call for the guard.

***

Leesee

I felt hot lips sucking all over my neck, and light groaning. The scent of a man's cologne went up my nose, intoxicating me. I popped my eyes open just as Sharome sucked on my earlobe as I lay on my side, feeling like the fattest chick in the world.

"Wake up, baby. I'm trying to hit some of that pregnant pussy. You know how good yo' shit been lately," he groaned, then squeezed my left breast just enough to let me know he was serious.

"Mm! Daddy, that hurt a li'l bit. You know they sensitive," I moaned, leaning back to expose more of my breast to him. I had fallen asleep in his Tom Ford button-up, and four of the buttons were undone already so I could breathe. He snuck his hand inside of it and pulled on my nipple, causing it to become erect before he got behind me and started to run his big dickhead up and down my moist slit.

"Uh! Daddy, what got you so riled up?" I asked, lifting my thigh so he could slide into me.

He placed my thigh on his forearm, holding it in the air before slamming forward, driving his dick deep into me from the side. I felt like I was being stuffed. He bit into the back of my neck and sucked on it, licking the top of my spine and sending chills all over my body.

"Uh! Uh! Uh! Daddy. Tell me. What. Got. You. So. Hot?" I moaned as he started to pound into me again and again. The sound of my wet pussy could be heard loud and clear. That noise alone was driving me crazy, and I found myself on the verge of cumming already.

He gripped my ass, smacked it, then pulled the cheeks apart while he drove into me. "I. Need. This. Body. Leesee! Ooh, shit. I. Missed. This. Pussy." He pulled me up and forced my face into the bed, along with the top of my pregnant belly. He fucked me hard from the back while he gripped my hips and smacked my big booty every ten strokes or so.

"Uh, Daddy! Daddy! Ooh! Fuck me, Daddy! I love it! I love this shit so much. Pull my hair! Pull it out my head!" I screamed.

He grabbed a fistful and yanked my head backward roughly, smacking my ass harder and driving forward like a savage. His fat, long dick opening me wider and wider, causing my walls to scream for more.

I could hear his heavy breathing behind me. My ass slammed backward into his lap again and again. I turned my head to the side and lay my cheek on the bedspread.

His thrusts grew more aggressive, driving me out of my mind.

"Uh, uh, uh, uh, ah, this shit so hot. This pussy real hot, ma. Ooh, this shit so good!" he moaned before leaning all the way forward and shooting his seed into my womb. I could feel it splashing and squirting all on my insides. The feel of it triggered my own orgasm as he continued to thrash me with force.

"Uh! Uh! Here I cum, Daddy. I'm cumming. I'm cumming all over this again. Ooh!" I screamed, squirting my juices all over him before falling to my side while he sucked all over my naked booty cheeks like he always did.

Twenty minutes later I sat in the tub while he sat on the edge of it and washed my back with a soapy towel, dunking it in my water before placing the towel on my shoulder blades and ringing it out. He leaned down and kissed my cheek. "You know I love you with all of my heart, right?" he asked, repeating the same washing process again and again.

I felt so relaxed and loved. I didn't think there was any man in the world who would do all of the things Sharome did for me. It was just like Tia said, he always tried his best to treat me like a princess. I was starting to see that more and more. I nodded my head. "Yeah, Daddy, I do. Why would you ask me that?"

He laid me back in the water, then began to wash my boobies before taking care of my big belly. Every time I saw it, I wondered how he really felt deep down in his heart. I wondered if seeing me with a pregnant belly made him feel some type of way.

He shrugged his shoulders as he ran the towel all over my belly, then replaced it with his bare hand, holding it still with a slight smile. "Nah, it ain't no cause for concern. I was just asking you because I know we had this thing a li'l while ago where we used to exchange *I love yous* all the time. Lately it's like we only say them every now and then, and even then they don't feel the same. At least not for me," he said, lowering his voice. He picked up the shampoo, squirting a nice portion into his hand before lathering it into my hair. He scratched my scalp to make sure he was getting up all of the dandruff that might have been there.

I closed my eyes and kept on replaying the words he'd just said to me. I was trying my best to not panic, but I needed to get an understanding as to what he really meant. So, as I felt him lean my head back, take the showerhead, and begin to wash the shampoo away, I had to get an understanding with him. "Baby, what are you saying? Are you saying you don't feel like our love is genuine anymore?" I opened my eyes so I could see his response.

He looked into them with his gray ones, then looked off, sighing and rolling his head around on his shoulders. "Close yo' eyes, Leesee, before you get shampoo in 'em," he ordered.

I closed them and frowned. "Okay, but I still need you to answer the question."

He exhaled loudly once again. "Yo, the last thing I'm trying to do is argue wit' you right now. I just got done getting me some of that li'l kitty, I'm in an okay mood, and I brought up a feeling I shouldn't have. It ain't no big deal."

I felt my blood pressure rising. "That don't answer the question, Sharome. Damn." I sat all the way up and grabbed the drying towel on the side of the tub, taking it and wiping my face. Then I took the showerhead out of his hand and rinsed the soap from the rest of my body.

Sharome got up and tried to reach out for me, I guessed to make sure I didn't fall, but I jerked my hand away from him. "I'm good, baby. You ain't gotta be alongside me every single step of the way. I ain't handicapped." I rolled my eyes and felt like crap as soon as I did it. I knew he was just trying to be a stand-up man, and I had a way of making it extremely hard for him, even when I didn't mean to.

He shook his head, turned his back on me, and left the bathroom. I watched him step into the room and sit on the bed with his head down, running his hands all over his face and mumbling to himself. I got out and dried myself off, wrapped the towel as far around my big belly as it would go, then made my way into the room.

"You know I hate when you do that shit, Sharome." I dropped the towel and grabbed my gown, sliding it over my head, then stepping in front of him with my arms crossed.

"What I do now, Leesee?" he asked, barely above a whisper. He kept his head lowered and looked at the floor wit' his eyes wide.

I sucked my teeth and slapped my hand on my hip, trying to calm myself down because I knew there was something bothering him, but he was the type to never really express what he was feeling in the moment. He'd always wait until things built up, then he'd decide to speak about them, and that irritated me so much. "Sharome, I can tell something is bothering you. Why won't you just tell me what it is so we can talk about it and move past it? Do you feel like our love is fake now? Or am I doing something that's throwing you off?" I asked, really wanting to know.

He shook his head and stood up, exhaling loudly. "Look, I'm just in one of my moods today. It really ain't got nothing to do wit' you. Far as our love goes, I mean, it is what it is. I still love you to death, and I'ma make sure I do everything I can to make sure you are always taken care of. It's not solely about me and you no more. There is another life that's more precious than the both of ours." He scratched his forehead and opened our closet door.

I stood frozen for a few seconds, still confused as to what he was really getting at. "What do you mean 'it is what it is' when it comes to our love? Are you saying from now on it's just going to be about this baby, and not you and I, or somethin'?" I asked, trying to imagine what that would even feel like. I wanted him to love me for me, not because of some child, whether it was ours or not.

He reached into his closet and grabbed a pair of purple-and-black Airmax, setting them next to the dresser. "To be honest with you, I don't know what I'm saying right now. My brain kind of fucked up. I know I got a whole bunch of responsibilities to take care of for you and Tia, and I gotta make shit happen. It's not gon' be easy supporting two children and two women, but you know what? It's the bed I've made. I gotta be a man about all of this shit. But I can't lie and say it ain't stressing me out a li'l bit. And lately you been catching an attitude about everything, even when I'm trying my best to do the right thing by you. No matter what it's never enough, and I guess I'm just tired, to say the least." He picked up the shoes and carried them down the hallway.

I stood there for a second, probably looking like a damn fool. I didn't know where all of this was coming from. I felt blindsided and a little hurt by it all. I made my way down the long hallway just as he was coming down it. He stopped mid-stride and looked me over. I bit into my bottom lip and blinked tears.

"Sharome, are you honestly saying you're tired of being with me or something? Has your love really changed for me? Be honest. All I need to hear is the truth in this moment."

He shook his head and brushed past me. "N'all, Leesee, I ain't saying that. All I'm saying is I been a li'l stressed out lately. Our circumstances are weighing heavy on my heart, and I'm just hoping I won't crack under the pressure, because ain't nobody feeding me emotionally other than Tia and them thirsty-ass broads out in Harlem that see me rising in the game. I don't get that love and affection from you, and you're supposed to be my woman. You're quick to tell me all of the things I am doing wrong, but you never dwell on all of the things I am doing right. It's one of the traits I dislike about you."

He walked into the room, opened the closet door, and knelt down, moving boxes out of the way before pulling his safe out and opening it. Once again I followed him, but this time with my head down. I watched him pull out three stacks of money and set them on the floor beside him before pushing the safe back into the closet and securing it. Then he leaned down and grabbed the money off the floor, thumbing through the bills.

I swallowed my spit. "I'm sorry I haven't been more supportive, Sharome. I know you're going through a lot, and you do everything you can to make sure no one in this house needs for anything. You are one hell of a man, and

I should tell you that more often. I promise I'll get better," I said, feeling low.

He waved me off. "Man, you good. Like I said before, I know what I gotta do. I appreciate everything you've said, but it's good, Leesee. I just gotta man the fuck up. It's just hard when I ain't never had a man in my life to teach me all the things I'm supposed to know already. Where am I supposed to get my strength from if my woman don't give it to me?" He shook his head.

I felt like he was taking low-key shots directly at me. The comment he'd made about Tia and the hoez out in Harlem had me heated. I felt like I was in competition with them, and it made me feel so fucking insecure.

He held the money up in his hand. "This fifty gees right here. I'm finna go upstairs and give this to Tia. I know you making her move out, and I just wanna make sure she good. No matter how we feel about her, she still has my kid in her womb. As a man, I gotta make sure she don't need for anything. I just wanted to let you know first," he said, tying a thick rubber band around the money.

I could no longer hold back my irritation, nor my emotions. Before I could say a word, tears were pouring out of my eyes. "You falling for that bitch, ain't you, Sharome?" I asked, walking into his face.

He turned his head and held me away at arm's length. "Man, shut that shit up. It ain't got nothing to do with that. What the fuck am I supposed to do? Huh?"

I knocked his arms out of the way and stepped closer to him, looking into his gray, angry eyes. "You already gave that bitch fifteen gees. Now you giving her another fifty? That's sixty-five. She don't need all of that. You just trying to spoil her like you be doing me, and I ain't going for it." I slapped the money out of his hand and across the room. "Fuck that bitch! You don't owe her nothing else. She ain't doing shit but playing yo' ass because you're so soft-hearted."

Sharome stood without saying a word for a long time, just looking at the floor in silence. Then he trained his grays on me and curled his upper lip. "Yo, on everything I love, Leesee, I'ma leave this house before you make me put my hands on you like one of them bitch-niggaz out there in that world." He walked across the room and picked up the money, then turned around to face me. "I love you, but you need to grow up and get a grip. All this shit you're doing ain't gon' do nothin' but destroy us." He shook his head and left the room.

I fell to my knees and broke down in tears, feeling like I was losing the best thing that ever happened to me.

Chapter 14

Rome

As I was on my way out of the house, Tia was just pulling up in her pink Benz truck. Soon as I stepped off the last step, she blew her horn and waved for me to come over. I walked over to her truck and stuck my head into the passenger's window, which was already rolled down. "What's good, li'l ma? How are you feeling today?" I asked, prayin' she was in a better mood than Leesee had been in.

She smiled and bit into her bottom lip all sexy-like. "I'm good. Just a li'l tired. Where are you headed?"

I shook my head. "I was just finna roll and get some air before I meet up wit' Ramsey tonight. I got a lot of shit on my mind that I gotta get off before then. Oh, and I got something for you, too."

She put her forefinger into her mouth and sucked on it. "What you got for me, baby?" I could see her eyes light up as if she was excited.

"Open the door and let's roll for a minute," I said, taking a step back and waiting for the door to pop. As soon as it did, I opened it and got out of the hot-ass sun. It was shining bright in the sky, and it felt like it was over a hundred degrees outside. I climbed into her passenger's seat and closed the door. The seatbelt automatically clicked around me. I waited for that to happen before I pulled it back a little bit and went into my pants pocket, grabbing the fifty thousand dollars and handing it over to Tia as she pulled away from the curb.

I looked to the house in time to see Leesee staring at us out of the window. Her eyes were wide open and looked a bit spooky.

Tia took the money and dropped it into her lap, her thick thighs on each side of it. "Why are you giving me this, Sharome? I still got the fifteen thousand you gave me a few days ago," she said, making a left at the end of the block and pulling into the busy intersection.

I reached and turned on her system. The smooth sounds of Jhene Aiko came cooing out of the speakers. Her voice was so calming to me. "I know you about to be moving out soon, and I just wanted to make sure you got everything you need. Nah mean?" I sat back and adjusted my seat a li'l bit. I needed more legroom.

She drove in silence for a brief moment, then looked over to me and smiled, her big belly poking out of her Gucci dress. I smiled at that. I knew our baby was going to be chocolate, probably just like her, and I was cool wit' that.

She shook her head. "Sharome, you can give me all of the money in the world, and I'll never be happy if you aren't my man. I love you so fucking much. You honestly need to know that, because I am going crazy knowing I have to leave that house without you by my side. I need you." She whispered the last part and inhaled, shaking her head before blowing it back out.

I saw her eyes were starting to water, and that made me feel some type of way. I honestly knew if I had met Tia before I had Leesee, then it was a good chance she and I would've wound up together and strong. She seemed like a real good woman, and I could tell she genuinely loved me. With Leesee, I think since she knew she had me wrapped up and under her control, she took me for granted a lot. I felt a person could never fully appreciate someone who is going hard for them every single day until they are at risk of losing that person, or they lose them altogether. Only then can they wake up and begin to see the light.

Tia sucked on her bottom lip. "So, how is this going to work out, Sharome? You know, when I move out and everything? What type of relationship will we have?"

She slowly pulled into the parking lot of the lakefront. It was already crowded with people, but it didn't take long for her to find a spot next to a family of Latinos who were pulling out a barbecue grill from their Ford Expedition. She pulled alongside them and a little Spanish girl, about the age of six, waved to her before running toward the sand with three other girls chasing behind her around the same age. Tia parked the car and turned off the ignition, leaving the radio playing smoothly in the background. Jhene Aiko sang about smoking the good-good sativa. I smiled and nodded my head at her track.

"I don't know how things gon' go after you move out, but what I want to let you know is, no matter what, I'm gon' be there for you whenever you need me, because I care about you, and I care about our baby you're carrying." I leaned over and kissed her stomach before rubbing it in a circular motion.

A part of me was ready to have a kid to love in the way my parents had never loved me. She'd already told me it was a boy, and I was excited for his arrival. I wanted to see a pure version of me. I wanted to be there for him from the moment he was pushed out of her womb. But I was also thinking about stacking my chips all the way up before he got there.

I lay my head on her stomach and rubbed, sniffing her up a li'l bit, smelling the scent of her perfume. In my opinion there was nothing more special than the woman who carried your child, which is why I always found myself at war with my own mind. I loved Leesee with all of my heart, and I knew I would never leave her under any circumstances, but the fact she was pregnant with Savan's kid often got to me. It made me feel powerless and second-class, whereas whenever I thought about Tia and her carrying my child, it made me feel happy. I also felt feelings for her I was desperately not trying to feel, but it was so hard because she made things between us so easy and relaxed. She was drama-free, and every time she was around me she let me know how much she loved me and how much she wanted to be with me. As a man, that made me feel strong and secure.

She rubbed the side of my head, then my cheek. "I just want a small portion of you, Sharome. I just want you to see me and know I love you with all of my heart, know I'll ride for you, that I will kill for you because you mean the world to me." She sniffled, and I was afraid to look up and into her crying face. I already felt emotional because of her always knowing the right things to say to me. I was trying to keep it together and be a man, or at least behave in the way I thought a man should. I didn't know if I was or not because no man had taken the time to teach me anything. I pretty much figured life out on my own, and that sucked.

"Do you hear me, Sharome? I love you so much, baby. Can you tell me you feel the same way? Please?" she whimpered.

I lifted my head and looked into her brown eyes, reaching to wipe her tears away. I couldn't get over the fact she was so damn fine to me, even now with her chubby chocolate cheeks and slightly wider nose. I had to smile at just her beauty alone.

I rubbed her cheek before holding it with my right hand. "Tia, I love you, baby. I love you, and I know for a fact you love me just as much. I feel it, ma. Every time you and I are in the same room, I feel it. I feel the same things you feel, and I just wish things were different, because if they were, then you and I would be together for the rest of our lives. I truly believe that."

A tear fell out of her eye, and I wiped it away with my thumb. She nodded her head. "But what about now? Why can't I have a piece of you right now? You're my every-thing. The father of my only child-to-be, and I should have my share of you. I deserve it. Do you have any idea how bad men have treated me my entire life, baby? Huh?" She blinked, and now she was crying as if she was at a funeral of a close loved one.

I continued to wipe away her tears and hold her face. "N]all, ma, I don't. But if you're willing to talk about it, I'm here to listen to you speak your heart. Then I'll shelter you, Tia, as much as I can. I promise."

She shook her head. "Sharome, ever since I was a lit-tle girl, nobody has ever given a fuck about me. Not even my own mother. But how could she when she was always doped up on heroin?" She lowered her head and broke down.

I came out of my seat and knelt down beside her, pull-ing her to my chest as the family outside spoke loudly in Spanish. "Baby, it's okay. Talk to me. I'm here, and I'm not going nowhere." I rubbed her back as she struggled to calm down.

"When I was little, Sharome, my mother used to allow men to take advantage of me as long as they paid her in dope. Can you imagine a little girl being forced to please grown men while her mother sat across from her and shot heroin into her veins, never once stopping to help me? And they hurt me so, so bad." She lowered her head onto my shoulder and sobbed loudly.

I found myself feeling empathetic and pissed off at the same time, imagining what she'd been through in her earlier years of life. It wasn't fair. No little girl should've had to experience the things she'd gone through. I felt like I wanted to go back in time and kill all of those men and pay somebody to smack the shit out of her mother. It made me think about my own crappy childhood. Through her revelations, I started to feel even more connected to her.

She shook her head. "Then my father never cared about me, either, Sharome. One day, when I was just eleven years old, I told him about the things my mother allowed men to do to me, and you know what he said?" she asked, raising her head and looking into my eyes.

I shook my head. "N'all, ma, what did he say?"

She wiped snot from her nose as it trailed down to her lip. "He said, 'well, since you already know what grown dick feel like, I might as well get my turn, too.' Then, for the next three days, he raped me over and over again until he couldn't get himself up down there. That was the last time I'd seen my father, because two days after that he was murdered by one of the men my mother owed money to."

I held her more firmly to my chest and continued to rub her back. "Baby, where is your mother now?" I asked, simply curious.

She shrugged her shoulders. "I don't know. I haven't seen or heard from my mother ever since I was fourteen years old. It was around that time I'd run away from home, but it was rumored she was murdered by the same man that took my father out of the game. But I don't know for sure. Sharome, the reason I am telling you this is because I need you to know what your love means to me, and what I stand to lose if you take it away from me. I'm not like Leesee. I never had a chance. No one ever cared about me until you stepped into the picture. Do you know the only reason I tried that heroin shit is because I wanted to see what was so special about it for my mother? How could a drug be so strong it would cause you to neglect your own child, or stand by while grown-ass men assaulted her? I didn't understand. But now, when I feel at my lowest point and I need some form of an escape, it's my only go-to option." She lowered her head. "I'm so screwed up. I can't take care of this baby without you being beside me twenty-four hours a day. I'm too weak. Always have been."

I shook my head and pulled her face down so I could kiss her lips ever so lightly. There was nothing sexual about the kiss. It was simply meant to heal her, to let her know I was there and I had her back, no matter what. Her story allowed me to see her in a completely different light. So we pecked, then I broke our kiss and looked her in the eyes.

"My mother didn't love me, either, Tia. She hated me because of the man who'd gotten her pregnant." I exhaled loudly. "My whole life I tried to do everything I could to please my mother, to make her happy or get her to see I was worthy of her love, but no matter what I did, nothing ever worked. She left this earth hating my guts, and I didn't make it any better because when it came down for me to choose between her or Leesee and both of their lives were on the line, I chose your cousin, and my mother's life was lost. So you see, there are things I hold deep within myself as well. My closet is so cluttered at times I can't breathe. Leesee is the reminder of my past choices. To not be with her is to basically say my mother died in vain." I lowered my head and shook it. "I'm so fucked up behind all of that, and I don't know what to do or which way to turn. I love her with all of my heart, Tia, but that baby inside of her is killing me, and I don't know how to get around it." I felt my throat getting tight and my eyes burning. Tears were already falling down my cheeks, but I hurried and wiped them away, clearing my throat and sitting up.

Tia grabbed my face into her small hands and kissed my lips. "You and I have so much in common, Sharome. I don't think it's by happenstance that we are having this baby together. I think we were meant to be together, and we need to embrace that." She lay her forehead against mine. "I love you with all of me. I will always love you in that way, and nothing or nobody will change that. You're the sweetest love I've ever known, and to let you go would be suicide for me. I mean that." She smiled and brushed her nose against mine.

I exhaled loudly and saw Leesee's face in my mind. "Things are going to be so difficult, though. I don't know how we're going to get through it, but we will. I feel like all we have to do is work hard at making these relationships work. That's important."

Tia nodded her head. "I'm willing to do everything I need to do to make you happy, Sharome. You'll never have to worry about me not staying in my lane. All I care about is never losing you or the love you have for me. Okay?" She kissed my lips again.

I smiled and pulled my head back so I could look into her brown eyes. "Yeah, ma. Just know I love you just as much as you do me. I'll always have your back, even though I'm with Leesee. I gotta be faithful and one hunnit to her, but it doesn't mean I won't be there for you. I promise."

Tia shook her head. "You just don't get it, and I don't think you ever will."

I wanted to ask her to elaborate, but her phone started to ring. She broke our embrace and looked at the screen before a worried look came over her.

Jelissa

Chapter 15

Leesee

Nine o'clock at night and Sharome and Tia were just pulling up to the house, even though they'd left together at around eleven o'clock. I was so fucking mad I felt like grabbing one of Sharome's guns from under the bed and unloading on the both of them. I felt like a damn fool. How could he spend so much time with her while I sat at home and cried my eyes out, wondering if he still loved me in the way he had before we left New Jersey? I continued to look out the window and got even more mad when I saw them exit her truck. She walked around the front of it and hugged him for way too long before he walked over to his Range Rover, got in, and pulled off, tapping the horn one time before disappearing down the street. Tia stood in place with a smile on her face, looking down the street until I guessed she could no longer see his whip. Only then did she make her way up the stairs.

I closed the curtain and had to jog to my room and close the door to calm myself or I really was going to kill this chocolate bitch. I paced back and forth, feeling my baby kick inside of me and my heart pound in my chest.

I heard the front door close, followed by her footsteps ascending the stairs. This bitch had the nerve to be singing to herself all joyful and shit like she was the happiest person in the whole wide world. That really had me fuming. I continued to pace and pace. I wondered if Sharome had fucked her pregnant pussy like he'd done mine earlier that day. Did they really have a secret relationship going on outside of me? What could they have possible done for ten hours straight together? They had to have fucked. It was the only thing that made sense.

I swung at the air and continued to pace until I couldn't take it no more. I got so irritated that I flipped up our bed, exposing the handguns under the mattress and picking up the all-black nine-millimeter Sharome had shown me how to shoot. I cocked it back and checked to make sure there was one in the chamber. After confirming there was, I put the gun in the small of my back like I'd often seen him do and made my way up the stairs.

I was ready to put an end to this bitch. The only way I could get Sharome to love me was if she was no longer in the picture. He was just one of those men who had to take care of anyone close to him. Tia took that and used it against him. He didn't see it, but I did.

So I made my way up to her room with murder on my mind.

***

Tia

I set the fifty thousand dollars on my dresser and smiled to myself as the cramping started again, deep within the pit of my stomach. My head began to hurt, and I felt sick. I needed a fix. I needed to feed my veins, or I was about to pass out from withdrawal. I pulled open the top dresser drawer, moved my panties to the side, and pulled out my works, consisting of my syringe, heroin, rug, spoon, and lighter. They were all conveniently placed inside a Ziploc bag.

I knelt down on the floor and took everything out. Once they decorated the carpet alongside my bed, I picked up the spoon and poured a hefty portion of heroin onto it, reaching onto the night table and grabbing my bottle water. I pouring a few drops of it onto the drug before lighting the bottom of the spoon. My phone rang at the same time I was drawing the dope into the syringe. I finished with my task, then answered it, placing it on speakerphone while I wrapped the tan cord around my bicep.

"Talk to me, Gino. I can hear you, baby," I said after seeing his picture pop up on the face of my phone. I set it down next to me as I stabbed my vein with the needle, pushing it deeply into me before squirting the drug into my system. My eyes fluttered as I was met with a rush of euphoria.

"Tia, where the fuck are you, baby? I thought you'da been back by now!" Gino hollered into the phone. I could tell he was upset. He'd been let out of jail early that morning, and I'd paid for a room so he could lay low until we figured out our next move. I had intended on coming back to the house to get some peace of mind away from him for a few hours, but then I'd been thrown off course by Rome's fine ass.

I smacked my lips together and closed my eyes, pulling the syringe from my veins and placing it back onto the dresser. I felt like a million bucks. I couldn't stop smiling. I missed Sharome already, but I knew I had to say something to make Gino feel better or I was in trouble.

"Baby, I know I been gone for a li'l while, but I had to meet up with that trick nigga I was telling you about. You know, to make sure everything is still on the up-and-up."

"And?" he hollered. "Is it? When am I knocking this nigga off? I feel like you playing games, Tia. Don't let me find out you fell in love with this victim. That'd get you and his punk-ass kilt, right after I cut my baby up out of you. Did you fuck him again?" he hollered.

I was in a zone. My whole body felt numb, and my pussy was throbbing even imagining Sharome fucking me. It seemed like every time I did heroin it made me so horny I could barely think straight. I had to snap out of it or I was going to fuck around and lose my life to Gino.

"N'all, baby. I told you, I ain't doing that no more. I'm not gon' fuck another man with your baby inside of me. Only hoez get down like that. You know me better than that," I said, though I didn't mean a word of it. Had Sharome wanted to lay me on my back, I would have broken my neck to give him what he wanted. I was obsessed with him and felt I always would be.

"Then why the fuck have you been gone so long? What could have taken you all day to do with this nigga?" he roared.

"Gino, we were on bidness, and he gave me another thirty thousand dollars, baby. You already know I'm finna bring that right to you," I said, keeping the other twenty Sharome had given me a secret. I needed to start to tuck away money, because as soon as I saw an opening to get away from Gino after he robbed Sharome, I was out of there. I knew without a shadow of a doubt that if I didn't, one day he would kill me.

Gino was quiet for a spell. "Thirty gees, huh? Must I remind you again about how much money is on your head? That shit you talking is peanuts, and I want that three hunnit bands you been telling me about. I'm tired of waiting, Tia. I see I'ma have to take matters into my own hands. Is that what you want me to do?" he asked.

I looked up as a shadow was cast over me and damn near shitted on myself. There was Leesee with a gun aimed directly at me and a scowl on her face. She stepped forward and put the barrel to my cheek, picking up the phone at the same time.

"Tia! Tia! Bitch, do you hear me? Huh?" Gino hollered at the top of his lungs. "You know what, bitch, I'm a block away. I'm finna –"

Leesee took the phone and threw it against the wall. "You dirty-ass bitch. I should have known that wasn't Sharome's baby. You always been a project ho, opening your legs for every nigga that moved a pack, just like yo' ratchet-ass mama!" she yelled.

I tilted my head back as she pressed the gun harder into my cheek. "Leesee, I swear it's not what you think. You walked up at the wrong time. What you heard was me trying to finesse this nigga that's been stalking me. I didn't mean any of it," I lied and prayed she believed me.

She reached out and smacked me across the face. I screamed and fell backward, landing on my works, the spoon digging into my back. I felt my lip already swelling up as if it was a balloon.

"And you in here doing heroin? Bitch, what the fuck is the matter with you?" she hollered, walking over to the dresser and holding up my money. "Did Sharome stupid-ass give you this? Huh? Was he the one you talking about on the phone? The so-called victim?" She scrunched her face and threw the money at me. It crashed into my face and went all over the place.

I reached and pulled the spoon out of my back just as there was the sound of a window breaking downstairs. This made Leesee perk up and look out into the hallway. I don't know what I was thinking, but in the moment she took her eyes off me, I jumped up and ran at her full-speed, tackling her into the wall in the hallway. She dropped her gun, and it slid across the carpet and stopped right at the top of the stairs. I took my mouth and bit her right on the neck as if I was a pit bull.

"Ah! You sick-ass bitch! Get the fuck off of me!" she hollered, pushing me into the wall before we fell to the floor, struggling for position.

I pulled her hair and yanked her head harshly to the side before kneeing her in the pelvic region. She removed her hands from around my neck and fell backward, trying to hold her crotch.

"Ah! Tia! What the fuck?" She rolled onto her side and cried tears of pain.

I jumped up and looked down on her with no remorse. I hated her fucking guts. I hated her because I could never be to Sharome what she was to him. I hated her because all she'd ever done was judge me. I hated her because she could never understand all I had been through.

"I hate you, Leesee!" *Bam*! I kicked her in the back so hard she rolled over onto her stomach, wincing in pain.

I hopped over her and ran to retrieve the gun, thoughts of ending her life heavy on my mind. But just as I made it to the top of the stairs with my back turned to her, I felt something sweep my legs from under me. The next thing I knew, Leesee was on top of me and punching me repeated in the face with what felt like superhuman strength.

"You. Stupid. Bitch. How. Dare. You. Plot. On. My."

All of the sudden she stopped. I felt the blood pouring out of my nose and looked up into her face. Her eyes were wide with fright. She jumped off of me and started to walk backward down the hall. "Who the fuck are you? What are you doing in my house?" she hollered.

I sat up just in time to see Gino walk up the steps with two guns extended, aimed at her. "Bitch, get down on yo' knees or I'ma blow yo' head off. Now, bitch!"

Leesee held her hands in the air, then without warning shot into my bedroom and closed the door. I could hear the sound of the lock turning. "Tia, get that muthafucka out of my house! I'm calling Sharome right now!" she screamed through the door.

Gino jumped over me and began to ram his shoulder into the door with so much force. "Open this door, bitch! Open it up before I start shooting through it!" He slammed his shoulder into it over and over again until the door jam was starting to splinter.

I got to my feet and held my stomach. I felt a sharp pain in my left side, and it almost made me topple over. I walked up to Gino and put my hand on his shoulder. "Baby, calm down. That's making too much noise. The neighbors are going to hear you. Just –"

He turned around and backhanded me so hard I flew into the wall. "Bitch! Shut the fuck up! It's yo' fault I gotta go through all of this shit!" He picked me up and threw me into the wall again so hard I crashed into it face-first and landed on my ass. Then he was back at the door with his shoulder. "Open this door, li'l girl!"

I felt the blood pouring out of my nose. I held my hand up to it. It dripped into my palm, then spilled over the side of it. I opened my mouth so I could breathe. I felt like I was about to panic. I couldn't believe this was happening.

Doom, doom, doom! The door caved in, sending Gino along for the ride. He fell to his knees, then jumped up, looking around for Leesee.

She stood in the corner of the room, holding the metal baseball bat I kept in the closet in case of an intruder. "Come on, nigga. I ain't scared of you. If you gon' shoot me, then go ahead, but I swear to God when my man catch yo' ass, he gon' kill you. He gon' knock your fucking head off of your shoulders."

Gino smiled and turned his head to the side, looking her over in amusement. He raised both guns and turned them sideways. "Look, bitch, I don't know who the fuck you talking about, but ain't no muthafucka gon' do shit to me. What you is gon' do is empty them fucking safes so I can be on my way. So lower that bat and we can get on with this shit. If you don't do like I say, I'ma pop yo' ass. Now, that's my word. You betta ask Tia who the fuck I am. Save yo' life, 'cause right now you on the verge of losing it."

I ran into the room and brushed past him. "Please listen to what he saying, Leesee. Please, because he will kill you. This ain't a game," I whimpered, feeling the blood drip off my chin.

Leesee shook her head and held the bat more firmly, tears running down her cheeks. "How could you do this to us, Tia? How could you bring him here after all we've done for you?" She said the last part through clenched teeth, never taking her eyes off Gino.

Gino smiled once again, running the toe of his shoes through the money that was spread all across the floor. "Tia, shut the fuck up and tell this bitch one more time to drop that bat or I'm finna pop her. I ain't playing. I swear to God," he warned.

***

Leesee

I held the bat up and got ready to swing. I felt if I could make contact with his head, then he would be forced to drop the guns, and I had plans on picking them right up and emptying them into both of their asses. I hated my cousin for putting us in this position. I wished we had never taken her in.

She stepped forward once again with blood all over her face, bleeding like a stuck pig, her hands out in front of her in total submission mode. "Leesee, just give me the bat, and then we can go downstairs and open up Sharome's safe, take the money, and be on our way. There is no need for anybody to get hurt any further. I'm begging you to listen to me. Please, little cousin."

I hated this bitch even more for thinking it was going to be this easy. I'd rather die than roll over and give them our money. He looked like a dope fien', and since I caught her with a needle deep in her arm, I knew she was, too. I wasn't going. I didn't give a fuck what she said.

I held the bat over my head as my heart pounded in my chest, took a step forward, and swung it with all of my might just as Gino jumped backward and fired his gun, illuminating the room.

Jelissa

Chapter 16

Rome

I sat back on the couch as Vice Roy took the two suitcases full of money, picked them up, and plopped them on the table before Ramsey with a smile on his face. He unzipped them one-by-one and pulled them open, exposing bundles and bundles of cash.

"I told you, Ramsey, all I needed was for you to put your faith in me. That work you gave me a li'l while ago popped like hotcakes. Now this is the reward. Just like I promised," he said, picking up a few stacks and thumbing through them in Ramsey's face.

I moved about uncomfortably on Ramsey's couch. Even though the scene was taking place in front of me, for some reason I had a bad feeling something wasn't right, though I didn't know what it could possibly be. I picked the blunt up out of the ashtray and took four strong pulls off of it, before placing it back into the ashtray.

Ramsey looked over at Vice Roy before grabbing a suitcase and going through it. "Looks like you handled yo' bitness, kid. How much is here?" he asked, picking up two handfuls, and looking Vice Roy over closely. He sucked his teeth and replaced the money.

Vice Roy took a step back and pulled out a Cuban cigar, lighting the tip. Small, gray smoke clouds floated into the air. "That's four million altogether. I told you the next time I hollered at you I was gon' come on bitness. I got a few pa'tnas down in Philly that's trying to jump on board with that liquid meth shit. Say they wanna crystalize it theirselves. I told them I had the plug and it wouldn't be a problem. Long story short, two million is from me, and two is from them. Let's ball out." He stepped around the table and extended his hand to Ramsey.

Ramsey opened the other suitcase and ran his hands all over the money inside, nodding his head with a smirk on his face. "You say Philly, huh?"

Vice Roy nodded. "Yeah, I got niggaz out there that's trying to eat off the kid. We finally coming to the table together, and I feel like it's needed. Why, what's the matter wit' Philly?"

Ramsey grunted and curled his upper lip. "Let me ask you a question." He closed the suitcase and looked Vice Roy over closely.

Vice Roy continued to puff on his weed-filled cigar. "Go ahead, the floor is yours."

Ramsey walked around the table with a scowl on his face. "Them niggaz you fucking wit' out in Philly, they Bloodz?"

Vice Roy wiped his mouth and flared his nostrils. "Yo, I don't give a fuck what they is. It's all about that green for me," he said, smiling and taking three deep pulls off his cigar.

Ramsey nodded his head. "Yo, I don't fuck wit' them Philly niggaz cuz most of them be working for the Feds. The only way I can distinguish what's what is if they plugged with my mob. If a nigga ain't from New York, then they gotta be plugged with my Blood niggaz. That's the only way I can distinguish who's who. I told you that already, my nigga. And besides that, word from the inside is you're already down 4.5 million to the mob."

Vice Roy's eyes got bucked. He took the cigar and stubbed it out in the ashtray right next to me. Large chunks of reddish weed fell out of it. "Now, wait a minute, Ramsey. What I got going on with them niggaz ain't got shit to do wit' you. This here is a separate deal." He walked over to the table and started to zip up the suitcases.

Ramsey whistled. Seconds later two of his goons came through the den's door with Tech .9s in their hands and red rags covering half of their faces.

I still couldn't understand why Ramsey had chosen to do a drug deal at one of the mansion where his family laid their heads on occasion, but I would find out later it was the only way he could get Vice Roy to let his guard down enough to enter a trap with only one armed bodyguard. At that moment the big, bald-headed man sat across from me with his eyes wide. As he rose, so did I. The only difference was I was strapped, and he wasn't.

I upped the two Glock .40s and aimed them at him. "Check this out, homie. You need to lie on yo' stomach until our bosses figure this shit out. Let's go!" I ordered, moving the table that separated us out of the way and grabbing him by the shirt, flinging him to the floor.

Ramsey laughed and upped a Glock .40 of his own, pointing it at Vice Roy's head. "Yo, word is bond, I don't like you D.C. niggaz, kid. Most of you fuck-niggaz is gay. Y'all snakes, and you fuck wit' them alphabet boys. I got word to whack yo' punk-ass on sight, my nigga. What you got to say about that?" he asked with the right side of his lip curled.

Vice Roy frowned and looked Ramsey over with hatred. "So that's what you on, nigga? You call me all the way out here so you can pull this bullshit, then you call me and my city of killas shysty and say we fucking wit' twelve thousand." He sucked his teeth loudly. "Man, nigga, fuck you then, Blood. Word is bond. I ain't finna bow down or none of that shit. I'm about to grab my money and my niggaz from Philly's scratch and walk the fuck out of here, or you gon' put one in my dome. That's how that's gon' go."

He made a move to smack Ramsey's gun out of his hand, when one of Ramsey's goons stepped forward, slammed his Tech to the back of Vice Roy's head, and pulled the trigger.

Boom, boom, boom!

The back of Vice Roy's head exploded before he jerked in the air and fell to his knees, and then his face with a pool of blood around him.

Ramsey took a red rag out of his back pocket and wiped his face with it, smiling down at Vice Roy. He looked over at his goon. "That's good shit, li'l homie. Pick his ass up and get him the fuck out of here. Take him down to the funeral home and have my uncle cremate his bitch-ass."

I watched as his two goons snatched Vice Roy's body up and dragged him out of the den. They left a trail of blood behind, and the whole time Vice Roy's head was slumped toward his chest.

Vice Roy's bodyguard started to whimper on the floor under me. I kept my Glock trained on him. "Blood, what's good wit' homie right here?" I asked, cocking back my pistol, ready to splash this stud.

Ramsey walked over to me and slapped his hand on my shoulder. "Aw, he good. That's my li'l nigga I'm about to put in power out there in D.C. He fucking wit' us. Let him up," he said, laughin' to himself.

I took a step back, confused as hell. The bodyguard jumped up and dusted off his all-black Gucci fit. He reminded me of Rick Ross.

"Yo, you have any idea what I had to do to get kid to trust you?" he asked, laughing. "Word is bond, that nigga been afraid to come out here for days, man. I made it seem like there wasn't no threat. Kid'll be a'ight, it's Blood in, Blood out. Son was on that other shit, too. All that fuck-shit you was talking about with the gay shit, kid was wit' it." He shrugged his shoulders. "To each its own, though. Oh, and that was just his paper. He ripped off them Philly niggaz two weeks ago. You know Bonjo an' 'em? They been at his head ever since. It's good now, though. It's time for the kid to eat like you said I would, word is bond." He stepped in front of Ramsey and gave him a half-hug.

An hour later, the den was clean and Vice Roy's security guard was heading back to D.C. with fifty kilos of meth and a half-gallon of liquid meth with Ramsey's strict orders. Ramsey promised to be out there in a few weeks, when he would bring some of the soldiers from his Harlem chapter to set up shop. He promised Vice Roy's bodyguard, whose name I found out was Cutty, that he would put him all the way on and allow for his city to run under him.

Ramsey came back into the den just as I was putting the cleaning supplies away. He was smoking on a blunt, laughing to himself. "I told you, Sharome, this game can be cold, li'l homie. You can't trust nobody because in the blink of an eye your life can be over. You gotta watch everybody closely, even your moms if she was in the game. Nah mean?"

I nodded as I watched him take the two suitcases and zip them up. "Yo, what I don't understand is why you would handle some bitness like this in a place where you lay your head? That don't seem smart to me. But after knowing you for a while, I know you never do nothing without it making sense, so what's good?" I asked, trying to see things through his eyes.

I always tried my best to model him closely because deep down he was the only father figure I ever had. I looked up to him, and I wanted to be like him when I got deeper into the game. With two kids on the way, I had to make sure when I did something it made sense for the long haul. It was all about that paper for me. I had to make sure I would be able to provide for both children and women for as long as I was alive. Ramsey gave me a position in the game that was sure to make a lot of money, but there was no way I would survive inside it if I wasn't smart and didn't move strategically. He was the head, so I had to pay close attention at all times to his chess moves.

He shrugged his shoulders. "That fool Vice Roy is a goon, but at the same time he real cautious. The only way I was going to be able to catch him slipping was if I brought him to a place he knew I laid my head. That fool know I live by the rules of the streets, and the first rule is you're never supposed to shit where you lay. He just knew I never would, so it caused him to lower his defenses, especially when he saw my kids' bikes out on the lawn and shit," he snickered. "The game is cold, but it's fair." He picked up the suitcases and handed me one. "Come on, help me take these bitchez upstairs so I can put them in my safe. It's fifty gees in here for you, too. You already know I gotta make sure my li'l nigga is straight at all times."

I grabbed the suitcase from him and smiled. One thing I could say about the homie was he made sure I was good at all times, and I appreciated that to the fullest.

As I made my way out of the den and up the stairs behind him, I couldn't help but look around his mansion in a state of envy, with its white walls and marble floors. He had all sorts of expensive paintings of prolific black people all around the house. There was a Jacuzzi directly in the center of his living room, and on the wall was a projector screen, I imagined to play movies while he relaxed inside the hot tub. He had a roaring fireplace that took big logs of wood. The kitchen this wife cooked inside was massive. All of the appliances looked brand new. His stairs went in a spiral, and the carpet on them was also white and soft to the feet. There was a steady scent of frankincense in the air that made the home feel welcoming.

Once we got to the top of the stairs, we made our way down a long hallway, that had four rooms on each side of it where his children, on occasion, slept. There was a door open when I passed that allowed me to see the room was furnished with a big screen television, a huge bed, and four different video game consoles on the side of it. I could tell whichever child slept in that room never had to worry about Ramsey saying no to them. They were spoiled, as I imagined all three of his kids were.

Finally, we made it all the way to his master bedroom, where he plopped the big suitcase on his bed. "Put that one right there, son, and help me move this dresser out of the way so I can wheel this safe out," he ordered.

I sat my suitcase on the bed and walked beside him as we began the task of moving the dresser. It felt like it weighed a thousand pounds, but slowly and surely we were able to move it just enough for him to get behind it. Once there, he pulled a latch in the wall outward, and then a small trap door appeared. Minutes later I stood back and watched him open a safe that was two times the size of mine. As soon as it opened, my eyes bugged out of my head. I could clearly see the inside of the safe was stuffed with cash. It looked like he literally had to pound it inside of there.

He got up, grabbed a suitcase, and unzipped it, reached inside and counted out fifty thousand dollars. He tossed it on the bed beside the other suitcase. "That's you right there, li'l homie. You can do whatever you want with it, and it ain't got nothin' to do with what I'ma pay you at the end of the week. This just my way of saying I love you, kid. Word is bond." He grabbed me and gave me a half-hug, gripping the back of my head like most niggaz did in Harlem.

I hugged him back. "I appreciate you, pa, No doubt, it's all love," I said before breaking our embrace.

He grabbed the suitcase and started to load the money into the safe, forcing it inside with each bundle he placed in it. "This gon' be you someday, Sharome. Trust me, kid. You keep fucking wit' me and allowing me to put you up on game, you gon' be eating like this in no time. Mark my words on that." He smiled and grabbed another bundle.

Leesee's image came into my mind as I looked over all of the money he was stuffing inside the safe. I knew for a fact with cash like that I would be able to provide for her and our child, not to mention I'd be able to send her to school and open up a few legit businesses. Our child wouldn't have to worry about nothing. I could also make sure Tia was straight, and my child wit' her. She'd never have to worry about nothing, either. I'd be able to place both women and our children on my shoulders the way a man was supposed to.

"Yeah, Sharome, I see a lot of me in you, li'l homie. I can tell you 'bout that life. You're thirsty for knowledge, and you got a good head on your shoulders. The mob needs good niggaz like you, dope boys that will take this hustling shit to the next level. How many kids you say you got on the way, though?" he asked, stuffing in a bundle of cash.

I laughed. "I got two on the way. It's a li'l scary, too, but I'm pretty sure I'm up for the task," I said, rolling my head around on my neck. I didn't really know if I was, but one thing was for sure: there was no quit in me. I would give those women all I had and make sure our children were well off. I owed it to them to do so.

Ramsey looked at me from his knees. "Damn, you got a two-piece? Fuck, that's crazy." He shook his head and started to load the safe again. "Man, I'ma be honest with you, Sharome. Them kids cost. All that flashy shit you're used to, you ain't finna be able to do none of that for a while 'cause they gon' hit yo' pockets. Then how many baby mamas you got? I hope it ain't more than one."

I felt the sweat pouring down my back and into my waist. The way Ramsey was talking was making me a li'l nervous. "I got two, big homie, but it's good. So far I been handling everything. You know, doing whatever it takes to put food on the table and clothes on our backs. You putting me on helps a lot. I can never repay you, as much as I wish I could," I said, feeling some type of way for the homie.

He got up and grabbed the other suitcase off the bed and started unloading its contents into the safe. "Man, long as you keep watching my back, li'l bruh, we good. You ain't never gotta worry about nothing. I got you." He continued to load the safe.

I looked down the hallway, thinking I heard a noise or something. "Ramsey, who else in the crib besides us, big homie?" I asked, ready to go down the stairs and regulate some shit.

He shook his head. "Nobody. I don't trust no muthafucka to be around me while I'm handling my bitness but you. Why, you hear something?" he asked, getting ready to stand up.

Just then I saw his puppy making its way down the hall, sniffing the carpet along the way with its tail wagging like crazy. That was a relief, because my heart was pounding in my chest. I didn't know what to expect. I held my hand up. "Aw, shit, it's just Killa's bad ass coming down the hall," I laughed. "We good."

The dog made its way inside the room and walked over to Ramsey, sniffing along his ribs. He elbowed it and continued to put the money in the safe. "This li'l mutt get on my nerves. My daughters get whatever they want, Sharome. Even soft-ass mutts like this."

He stuffed the last bundle of cash into the safe and got ready to close it, but before he did he looked up at me and froze. I had tears running down my cheeks and snot oozing out of my nose along with my pistol pointed toward him, the hammer already cocked back.

He swallowed. "Li'l homie, this how you gon' do me? After all I've done for you? I thought you was my li'l nigga, man. You like my fucking son," he hollered.

I took a deep breath, nodded, and pulled the trigger three times. *Boom, boom, boom.* Killa ran out of the room, yelping down the hallway as Ramsey fell backward with blood oozing out of his head.

Minutes later I found myself coming from his kitchen with a big, black garbage bag before loading it with all of his money. The only thing on my mind was making sure I would be able to provide for my family for the long haul. We had to get out of New York. We had to be on the next thing smoking. There was no way around it. I felt sick for betraying the homie, but my babies had to come first. The future of our security lay solely on my shoulders. I don't know how many real men would have done things differently.

Jelissa

Chapter 17

Leesee

Gino's first bullet slammed into my shoulder and knocked me backward into the dresser. It felt like someone had poured acid on me and it melted through my skin. "Argh!" I screamed as the second bullet whizzed across my ear, taking the bottom piece of my earlobe along with it. I landed on my back, holding my wounded shoulder. Blood oozed through my fingers as the pain shot all through me.

Gino stood over me with the smoking gun. "Punk-ass bitch! I told you I ain't the one to be played with. Get yo' ass up!" He grabbed a handful of my hair and dragged me out of the room and down the stairs.

The pain was so bad from the bumps that I pissed on myself and didn't even know it until I got to the last step and Gino leaned down into my face with a frown. It was then I felt the wetness between my legs, my shoulder throbbing horribly. I immediately thought about the baby. *Did my water break? Did I miscarry? Lord, please let my baby be okay.*

"Now, listen to me carefully. We finna go in this room, and you gon' give me the combination to this safe, and I'ma be on my way. I don't wanna kill you, but if you play wit' me, I ain't gon' hesitate. You got that?"

Tears streamed down my face as the pain became almost too much for me to bear, I nodded my head. "Okay, Gino, you can have the money. But after that, get the fuck out of my house. You and that snake-ass bitch over there," I said, looking over his shoulder at Tia as she came down the stairs with Sharome's gun in her hand.

Gino leaned down and grabbed my shoulder right by the bullet wound and squeezed it with all of his might. I screamed at the top of my lungs, flopping around on the floor like a fish out of water. The pain was so intense I couldn't see straight. He grabbed me up by my hair and forced me into my and Sharome's bedroom, tossing me on the floor roughly. "Pull out that safe and open that bitch up. Now!"

I winced in pain, then slowly slid across the floor on my side. I could feel the baby kicking in my stomach and blood spurting out of my shoulder. I got into the closet and moved all of the shoeboxes out of the way. I peeled back the wall, exposing Sharome's safe, opened the panel, and put in the code. It flashed for a second and popped open.

As soon as it did, Gino yanked me out of the closet by my hair and threw me to the floor. "Baby, make sure this bitch don't move. And if she do, you put a bullet in her head, you got that?" he asked, mugging the shit out of Tia and me.

She stepped forward and put the gun to my head after throwing Gino two pillowcases I figured she'd snagged out of the linen closet in the hallway. "Don't worry, baby. And don't forget after you empty that one, she got a whole 'nother safe behind the dresser." She put her foot on my chest and kicked me backward.

"You ain't gon' get away with this, you dirty bitch," I screamed, out of breath. I was so dizzy I couldn't see straight.

Gino started to load the pillowcases with Sharome's money, mumbling to himself. "Damn, baby, you was right. This nigga loaded up." He laughed and kept on putting the money into the pillowcases until they were full, then he grabbed the sheet off the bed and added the rest of the money to it. Once he finished, he kicked me in the foot. "A'right, bitch, where this other safe at?"

I was so dizzy. I was seconds away from fading out. I saw two versions of him, and my shoulder felt like somebody was trying to rip it off.

He kicked me again.

"It's behind the dresser, Gino. Take it and go. The code is 8-23-15."

Gino nodded, walked over to the dresser, and tore it away from the wall. It fell on top of me, and nobody made a move to help me.

Just as I wiggled from under it, I heard the front door opening and closing. "Baby? Leesee, where you at, boo?" Sharome hollered.

Gino jumped back from my safe that he was unloading, leaned down, and placed his hand around my mouth. "Bitch, you betta not say nothing," he hissed. He pulled me backward until we were in the bathroom, where he closed the door.

***

Tia

I felt like I was going to throw up when I heard Sharome's voice. *Fuck, why did he have to come home while all of this was happenin'? Why couldn't he have stayed away?* I questioned the heavens above.

167

"Baby, you gotta get up and get dressed. We gotta get Tia and get the fuck outta here," he said, walking toward the room's door, which I'd closed.

I'd managed to slip into the guest bedroom about ten feet away from their actual room. My heart pounded in my chest. My breathing labored and sweat pouring down my forehead, I waited for him to walk past me. As soon as he did, I jumped out of the dark room with the gun raised, tears running down my cheeks. "Sharome! I'm so sorry."

He froze in his tracks, then turned around to face me at the same time the bedroom door swung open. His eyes were as big as saucers. "Tia, what the fuck are you doing, ma?"

Before I could answer him, Gino took over the show. "Sucka-fo'-love-ass-nigga! Don't you know to never trust a bitch?" *Boom. Boom. Boom. Boom.* The sparks from his gun lit up the dark hallway.

Sharome fell forward into my arms, his heavy body knocking me backward, smothering me. He jerked and shook, coughing up large globs of blood with his eyes wide open. Then all of a sudden he stopped and became still.

I pushed him off of me with tears in my eyes. Looking down at his deceased body, I felt bits of remorse. The only man who had ever loved me was no longer living. Set up by me. I felt like the devil, and I knew I would never meet his caliber of man ever again.

"Get yo' ass up and help me with this money," Gino ordered, going back into the room.

The bathroom door opened and Leesee came crawling out of it on her knees. "What did you do, Gino? What did you do to my baby?" she cried, out of breath.

168

Gino looked over to me and frowned. "Kill that bitch, Tia! Kill her right now. Hurry the fuck up!" he yelled.

I nearly tripped over my own feet running over to the bathroom as Sharome's blood slid down my chest and in between my cleavage. By the time I got to Leesee, she'd fallen onto her side, breathing heavily, her asthma probably getting the better of her.

I pointed the gun down at her. "I'm so sorry, cuz. I wish all of this never happened. I love you so much," I cried, feeling my knees go weak.

"Bitch, if I gotta tell you again!" Gino hollered.

I sniffed and closed my eyes after seeing Leesee curl into a ball. "I'm sorry."

Boom. Boom. Boom.

As soon as I released the bullets, I fell to my knees, weak from it all, all of the day's events almost too much for me to mentally process.

Gino walked over and looked down at Leesee's body with a scowl on his face. Then he shook his head. "One thing I can say about that li'l bitch is she had heart. Hm." He shook his head, then looked down to me. "Man, to be honest wit' you, Tia, I ain't ready for no kids. And if you'll do yo' cousin like this, then what the fuck will you do to me?" He upped his .38 special, put it to my face, and pulled the trigger.

Karma's a bitch.

The End

I hope you all enjoyed this series as much as I enjoyed writing it. I am open to any thoughts or ideas on how I can improve my pen game. As an Author, there's always room to improve. A sincere thank you goes to those who continue to rock with me, giving me a chance.

Please stay connected with me on either of my Facebook pages, Authoress Jelissa Shanté or Author Jelissa Edwards. Please feel free to join the "Feenin' For Fiction" Readers Group, as well as the "Mental Health Matters Support Family" Group. God bless.

Love Always,

Jelissa Shante

Submission Guideline

Submit the first three chapters of your completed manuscript to ldpsubmissions@gmail.com, subject line: Your book's title. The manuscript must be in a .doc file and sent as an attachment. Document should be in Times New Roman, double spaced and in size 12 font. Also, provide your synopsis and full contact information. If sending multiple submissions, they must each be in a separate email.

Have a story but no way to send it electronically? You can still submit to LDP/Ca$h Presents. Send in the first three chapters, written or typed, of your completed manuscript to:

LDP: Submissions Dept
Po Box 870494
Mesquite, Tx 75187

DO NOT send original manuscript. Must be a duplicate.

Provide your synopsis and a cover letter containing your full contact information.

Thanks for considering LDP and Ca$h Presents.

Coming Soon from Lock Down Publications/Ca$h Presents

BOW DOWN TO MY GANGSTA

By **Ca$h**

TORN BETWEEN TWO

By **Coffee**

BLOOD STAINS OF A SHOTTA **III**

By **Jamaica**

STEADY MOBBIN **III**

By **Marcellus Allen**

BLOOD OF A BOSS **VI**

By **Askari**

LOYAL TO THE GAME **IV**

LIFE OF SIN **III**

By **T.J. & Jelissa**

A DOPEBOY'S PRAYER **II**

By **Eddie "Wolf" Lee**

IF LOVING YOU IS WRONG… **III**

By **Jelissa**

TRUE SAVAGE **VII**

By **Chris Green**

BLAST FOR ME **III**

DUFFLE BAG CARTEL **IV**

By **Ghost**

ADDICTIED TO THE DRAMA **III**

By **Jamila Mathis**

A HUSTLER'S DECEIT 3

KILL ZONE **II**

BAE BELONGS TO ME III

SOUL OF A MONSTER II

By **Aryanna**

THE COST OF LOYALTY **III**

By **Kweli**

SHE FELL IN LOVE WITH A REAL ONE **II**

By **Tamara Butler**

RENEGADE BOYS **III**

By **Meesha**

A GANGSTER'S SYN II

By **J-Blunt**

KING OF NEW YORK V

RISE TO POWER III

COKE KINGS III

By **T.J. Edwards**

GORILLAZ IN THE BAY IV

De'Kari

THE STREETS ARE CALLING II

Duquie Wilson

KINGPIN KILLAZ IV

STREET KINGS 2

PAID IN BLOOD 2

Hood Rich

SINS OF A HUSTLA II

ASAD

TRIGGADALE III

Elijah R. Freeman

MARRIED TO A BOSS III

By Destiny Skai & Chris Green

KINGZ OF THE GAME III

Playa Ray

SLAUGHTER GANG II

By Willie Slaughter

THE HEART OF A SAVAGE II

By Jibril Williams

FUK SHYT II

By Blakk Diamond

THE DOPEMAN'S BODYGAURD II

By Tranay Adams

<u>Available Now</u>

<u>RESTRAINING ORDER **I & II**</u>

By **CA$H & Coffee**

<u>LOVE KNOWS NO BOUNDARIES **I II & III**</u>

By **Coffee**

<u>RAISED AS A GOON I, II, III & IV</u>

<u>BRED BY THE SLUMS I, II, III</u>

<u>BLAST FOR ME I & II</u>

<u>ROTTEN TO THE CORE I II III</u>

<u>A BRONX TALE I, II, III</u>

<u>DUFFEL BAG CARTEL I II III</u>

By **Ghost**

LAY IT DOWN **I & II**

LAST OF A DYING BREED

BLOOD STAINS OF A SHOTTA I & II

By **Jamaica**

LOYAL TO THE GAME

LOYAL TO THE GAME II

LOYAL TO THE GAME III

LIFE OF SIN I, II

By **TJ & Jelissa**

BLOODY COMMAS I & II

SKI MASK CARTEL I II & III

KING OF NEW YORK I II,III IV

RISE TO POWER I II

COKE KINGS I II

By **T.J. Edwards**

IF LOVING HIM IS WRONG…I & II

LOVE ME EVEN WHEN IT HURTS I II III

By **Jelissa**

WHEN THE STREETS CLAP BACK I & II III

By **Jibril Williams**

A DISTINGUISHED THUG STOLE MY HEART I II & III

LOVE SHOULDN'T HURT I II III IV

RENEGADE BOYS I & II

By **Meesha**

A GANGSTER'S CODE I &, II III

A GANGSTER'S SYN

By J-Blunt

PUSH IT TO THE LIMIT

By **Bre' Hayes**

BLOOD OF A BOSS **I, II, III, IV, V**

By **Askari**

THE STREETS BLEED MURDER **I, II & III**

THE HEART OF A GANGSTA I II& III

By **Jerry Jackson**

CUM FOR ME

CUM FOR ME 2

CUM FOR ME 3

CUM FOR ME 4

CUM FOR ME 5

An **LDP Erotica Collaboration**

BRIDE OF A HUSTLA **I II & II**

THE FETTI GIRLS **I, II& III**

CORRUPTED BY A GANGSTA I, II III, IV

By **Destiny Skai**

WHEN A GOOD GIRL GOES BAD

By **Adrienne**

THE COST OF LOYALTY

By Kweli

A GANGSTER'S REVENGE **I II III & IV**

THE BOSS MAN'S DAUGHTERS

THE BOSS MAN'S DAUGHTERS II

THE BOSSMAN'S DAUGHTERS III

THE BOSSMAN'S DAUGHTERS IV

THE BOSS MAN'S DAUGHTERS **V**

A SAVAGE LOVE **I & II**

BAE BELONGS TO ME I II

A HUSTLER'S DECEIT I, II, III

WHAT BAD BITCHES DO I, II, III

SOUL OF A MONSTER

By **Aryanna**

A KINGPIN'S AMBITON

A KINGPIN'S AMBITION **II**

I MURDER FOR THE DOUGH

By **Ambitious**

TRUE SAVAGE

TRUE SAVAGE II

TRUE SAVAGE **III**

TRUE SAVAGE **IV**

TRUE SAVAGE **V**

TRUE SAVAGE **VI**

By **Chris Green**

A DOPEBOY'S PRAYER

By **Eddie "Wolf" Lee**

THE KING CARTEL **I, II & III**

By **Frank Gresham**

THESE NIGGAS AIN'T LOYAL **I, II & III**

By **Nikki Tee**

GANGSTA SHYT **I II &III**

By **CATO**

THE ULTIMATE BETRAYAL

Jelissa

By **Phoenix**
BOSS'N UP **I , II & III**
By **Royal Nicole**
I LOVE YOU TO DEATH
By Destiny J
I RIDE FOR MY HITTA
I STILL RIDE FOR MY HITTA
By **Misty Holt**
LOVE & CHASIN' PAPER
By **Qay Crockett**
TO DIE IN VAIN
SINS OF A HUSTLA
By **ASAD**
BROOKLYN HUSTLAZ
By **Boogsy Morina**
BROOKLYN ON LOCK I & II
By **Sonovia**
GANGSTA CITY
By **Teddy Duke**
A DRUG KING AND HIS DIAMOND I & II III
A DOPEMAN'S RICHES
HER MAN, MINE'S TOO I, II
CASH MONEY HO'S
By Nicole Goosby
TRAPHOUSE KING **I II & III**
KINGPIN KILLAZ I II III
STREET KINGS

PAID IN BLOOD

By **Hood Rich**

LIPSTICK KILLAH **I, II, III**

CRIME OF PASSION I & II

By **Mimi**

STEADY MOBBN' **I, II, III**

By **Marcellus Allen**

WHO SHOT YA **I, II, III**

Renta

GORILLAZ IN THE BAY **I II III**

DE'KARI

TRIGGADALE I II

Elijah R. Freeman

GOD BLESS THE TRAPPERS I, II, III

THESE SCANDALOUS STREETS I, II, III

FEAR MY GANGSTA I, II, III

THESE STREETS DON'T LOVE NOBODY I, II

BURY ME A G I, II, III, IV, V

A GANGSTA'S EMPIRE I, II, III, IV

THE DOPEMAN'S BODYGAURD

Tranay Adams

THE STREETS ARE CALLING

Duquie Wilson

MARRIED TO A BOSS… I II

By Destiny Skai & Chris Green

KINGZ OF THE GAME I II

Playa Ray

SLAUGHTER GANG II

By Willie Slaughter

THE HEART OF A SAVAGE

By Jibril Williams

FUK SHYT

By Blakk Diamond

<u>BOOKS BY LDP'S CEO, CA$H</u>

<u>TRUST IN NO MAN</u>
<u>TRUST IN NO MAN 2</u>
<u>TRUST IN NO MAN 3</u>
<u>BONDED BY BLOOD</u>
<u>SHORTY GOT A THUG</u>
<u>THUGS CRY</u>
<u>THUGS CRY 2</u>
<u>THUGS CRY 3</u>
<u>TRUST NO BITCH</u>
<u>TRUST NO BITCH 2</u>
<u>TRUST NO BITCH 3</u>
<u>TIL MY CASKET DROPS</u>
<u>RESTRAINING ORDER</u>
<u>RESTRAINING ORDER 2</u>
<u>IN LOVE WITH A CONVICT</u>

Coming Soon
BONDED BY BLOOD 2
BOW DOWN TO MY GANGSTA

Jelissa